***What was s[he] [doing with]
Justice Wilder, letting him kiss her?***

This was exactly what she had to *avoid*.

She'd started this, and she had to end it, before she melted into his arms and things got completely out of control.

In the end, they both pulled back at the same moment.

Kelly pressed trembling fingers to her lips, as if to keep the memory of his kiss there forever.

"I'm sorry," she whispered, not sure quite what it was she was apologizing for.

"Forget it," Justice said, his voice as curt and unemotional as ever. "It won't happen again."

But Kelly knew she'd *never* forget that kiss, not if she lived to be a hundred and fifty years old....

Dear Reader,

Summer is over and it's time to kick back into high gear. Just be sure to treat yourself with a luxuriant read or two (or, hey, all six) from Silhouette Romance. Remember—work hard, play harder!

Although October is officially Breast Cancer Awareness month, we'd like to invite you to start thinking about it now. In a wonderful, uplifting story, a rancher reluctantly agrees to model for a charity calendar to earn money for cancer research. At the back of that book, we've also included a guide for self-exams. Don't miss Cara Colter's must-read *9 Out of 10 Women Can't Be Wrong* (#1615).

Indulge yourself with megapopular author Karen Rose Smith and her CROWN AND GLORY series installment, *Searching for Her Prince* (#1612). A missing heir puts love on the line when he hides his identity from the woman assigned to track him down. The royal, brooding hero in Sandra Paul's stormy *Caught by Surprise* (#1614), the latest in the A TALE OF THE SEA adventure, also has secrets—and intends to make his beautiful captor pay…by making her his wife!

Jesse Colton is a special agent forced to play pretend boyfriend to uncover dangerous truths in the fourth of THE COLTONS: COMANCHE BLOOD spinoff, *The Raven's Assignment* (#1613), by bestselling author Kasey Michaels. And in Cathie Linz's MEN OF HONOR title, *Married to a Marine* (#1616), combat-hardened Justice Wilder had shut himself away from the world—until his ex-wife's younger sister comes knocking.… Finally, in Laurey Bright's tender and true *Life with Riley* (#1617), free-spirited Riley Morrisset may not be the perfect society wife, but she's exactly what her stiff-collared boss needs!

Happy reading—and please keep in touch.

Mary-Theresa Hussey

Mary-Theresa Hussey
Senior Editor

Please address questions and book requests to:
Silhouette Reader Service
U.S.: 3010 Walden Ave., P.O. Box 1325, Buffalo, NY 14269
Canadian: P.O. Box 609, Fort Erie, Ont. L2A 5X3

Married to a Marine

CATHIE LINZ

SILHOUETTE *Romance*®

Published by Silhouette Books

America's Publisher of Contemporary Romance

If you purchased this book without a cover you should be aware that this book is stolen property. It was reported as "unsold and destroyed" to the publisher, and neither the author nor the publisher has received any payment for this "stripped book."

Acknowledgments

Special thanks to Julie Murphy, P.T., for answering my questions about physical therapists, and to Cleo Pappas from the Lisle Public Library. This book is dedicated to the families of the men and women in our armed forces.

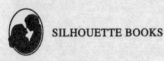

SILHOUETTE BOOKS

ISBN 0-373-19616-4

MARRIED TO A MARINE

Copyright © 2002 by Cathie L. Baumgardner

All rights reserved. Except for use in any review, the reproduction or utilization of this work in whole or in part in any form by any electronic, mechanical or other means, now known or hereafter invented, including xerography, photocopying and recording, or in any information storage or retrieval system, is forbidden without the written permission of the editorial office, Silhouette Books, 300 East 42nd Street, New York, NY 10017 U.S.A.

All characters in this book have no existence outside the imagination of the author and have no relation whatsoever to anyone bearing the same name or names. They are not even distantly inspired by any individual known or unknown to the author, and all incidents are pure invention.

This edition published by arrangement with Harlequin Books S.A.

® and TM are trademarks of Harlequin Books S.A., used under license. Trademarks indicated with ® are registered in the United States Patent and Trademark Office, the Canadian Trade Marks Office and in other countries.

Visit Silhouette at www.eHarlequin.com

Printed in U.S.A.

Books by Cathie Linz

Silhouette Romance

One of a Kind Marriage #1032
*Daddy in Dress Blues #1470
*Stranded with the Sergeant #1534
*The Marine & the Princess #1561
A Prince at Last! #1594
*Married to a Marine #1616

Silhouette Books

Montana Mavericks
"Baby Wanted"

*Men of Honor
†Three Weddings and a Gift

Silhouette Desire

Change of Heart #408
A Friend in Need #443
As Good as Gold #484
Adam's Way #519
Smiles #575
Handyman #616
Smooth Sailing #665
Flirting with Trouble #722
Male Ordered Bride #761
Escapades #804
Midnight Ice #846
Bridal Blues #894
A Wife in Time #958
†Michael's Baby #1023
†Seducing Hunter #1029
†Abbie and the Cowboy #1036
Husband Needed #1098

CATHIE LINZ

left her career in a university law library to become a *USA TODAY* bestselling author of contemporary romances. She is the recipient of the highly coveted Storyteller of the Year Award given by *Romantic Times* and was recently nominated for a Love and Laughter Career Achievement Award for the delightful humor in her books.

Although Cathie loves to travel, she is always glad to get back home to her family, her various cats, her trusty computer and her hidden cache of Oreo cookies!

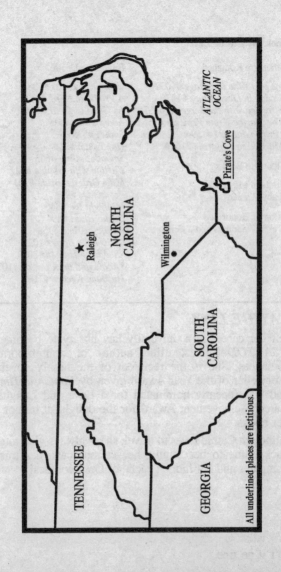

ATLANTIC
OCEAN

Pirate's Cove

NORTH
CAROLINA

★ Raleigh

Wilmington

SOUTH
CAROLINA

TENNESSEE

GEORGIA

All underlined places are fictitious.

Chapter One

Lightning flashed against the distant night sky and reflected on the dark water. "You sure you're expected?"

Kelly Hart nodded at the fisherman she'd hired to take her from the small North Carolina coastal town out to the island known as Pirate's Cove. The impending thunderstorm didn't bother her. She doubted it could hold a candle to the storm of protest U.S. Marine Justice Wilder would generate when he saw her.

It was fitting that Justice had holed up on a place called Pirate's Cove. There had always been something of a renegade about him, something dangerous and sexy.

"Don't worry about me," Kelly said. It was something she said often. At twenty-eight, she'd grown into the kind of woman who could take care of whatever came her way, even a furious Marine. "I'll be fine."

She repeated the words to herself as she hauled the provisions she'd brought with her the short distance from the beach to the only house visible from the boat dock. There was a single light on inside. Kelly heard the first distant boom of thunder as she pounded on the door.

It was yanked open a moment later.

And there he was. Justice Wilder. Looking none too pleased to see her. And looking far better than a man in his condition should look. But a second glance showed the paleness of his face, the lines of pain around his mouth, the cuts and bruises on his muscular legs, the sling holding his right arm.

His dark hair tumbled over his forehead. It was longer than when she'd seen him last. He was wearing military-green boxers and a T-shirt emblazoned with the USMC logo. He'd barely been twenty that last time she'd seen him. He'd made her heart pound then, and he had the same effect now.

She drank in the sight of him. His lean cheeks, his tempting mouth, his tall ranginess. The teenager had grown into a man—a man who still had the power to go straight to her heart. It was amazing. Even after all this time, even under these conditions, she still felt a zing.

He apparently did not. His blue eyes were dark with fury as he glared at her. "What the Sam Hill are you doing here?"

Marines don't swear, he'd once told her. Swearing shows a lack of discipline.

His words snapped her out of her reverie. Making the most of the Southern accent she'd acquired during her time in Nashville, Kelly drawled, "I heard you were having a pity party for yourself and I decided to come join you.''

Justice appeared taken aback by her blunt reply.

Good. She wanted to jar him out of whatever idiocy was preventing him from taking care of himself and his injuries properly. He had no right to make his poor mother so frantic with worry. Not to mention that he had no right to look so sexy that her knees were mushy.

''Do I know you?'' he demanded.

Okay, so the guy hadn't seen her since she was an awkward teenager, and even then he'd barely noticed her. She just somehow hadn't prepared herself for the possibility that he wouldn't recognize her.

Did she look that disheveled? Sure the cargo pants she wore were wrinkled from the trip, but the lime-green T-shirt she'd teamed with them usually looked fine on her. Her light-brown hair was gathered up into a braid to avoid being messed up by the increasing wind. She didn't have the kind of memorable looks that her sister possessed. She didn't even have her sister's gorgeous blue eyes. Instead Kelly had brown eyes.

But then, she hadn't come here looking to win any beauty contests. She'd come here to help Mrs. Wilder by helping her oldest and most stubborn son.

Kelly hadn't seen Justice in years. She wouldn't be coming to see him now were it not for the desperate phone call she'd received from his mother yesterday morning. She replayed the conversation in her head.

''Kelly, I need your help. I wouldn't ask if there was any other way...'' The older woman's voice had cracked with emotion.

"You know I'll help you any way I can," Kelly had assured her. "What's wrong?"

"It's Justice," Mrs. Wilder replied. "He's hurt. He saved a little boy in a car accident but was badly injured in the process. It happened near the Marine base here in North Carolina a week ago. After staying overnight, Justice checked himself out of the hospital first thing this morning. I couldn't stop him. But I made him tell me where he's going. To a friend's beach house. I want you to talk him into getting the physical therapy he needs. And I'll be honest with you, Kelly, that may mean giving it to him yourself. I know this is an awkward situation…" Mrs. Wilder's voice trailed off. They never really referred to it—the divorce between Kelly's older sister, Barbie, and Mrs. Wilder's oldest son, Justice—as anything other than the "awkward situation."

Some might find it strange that Kelly had developed such a close relationship with Mrs. Wilder, a relationship that continued even after Barbie had dumped Justice. But they didn't know the facts, or the emotions.

Kelly had only been thirteen when her mom died in a train accident and her older sister married Justice right out of high school. Mrs. Wilder had been a godsend to Kelly at that time, taking the gangly Kelly under her wing and mothering her with love and support.

The marriage between Barbie and Justice had only lasted two years, but the close bonds between Mrs. Wilder and Kelly had continued on for a decade and had strengthened. Mrs. Wilder had helped Kelly pick out a high school prom dress, had listened to her worries about attending an out-of-state college, had encouraged her to follow her dream of becoming a physical therapist, had agreed the job opportunity in Nashville was too good to let pass.

Mrs. Wilder had been there for Kelly at a time when she'd really needed a motherly influence, and she'd continued to be there for her throughout the years. Kelly would walk through fire for her.

"I hate to ask you," Mrs. Wilder had said unsteadily. "But I don't know what else to do."

Kelly had known what to do. The right thing, the only thing to do. Help Mrs. Wilder any way she could.

And so here she was. Coming to the rescue. The question was how to do that? Justice didn't recognize her. Should she let him know who she was right away? Her relationship to Barbie was hardly likely to put her on the top of his guest list.

She was considering her options when something clicked and Justice's gaze hardened.

"I'm Kelly," she said, even though she could tell he'd already gathered that much. "Kelly Hart. Your mother sent me."

Justice looked as if he didn't believe a word she was saying. Meanwhile the thunder was rumbling closer and closer. "Why would my mother do that?"

"Because she knows I'm a physical therapist." Kelly was not about to reveal the ongoing friendship she had with Mrs. Wilder to Justice yet. She doubted he'd understand.

"Go away. I don't want you here," Justice growled.

"I did rather get that impression," she noted wryly.

"You can't stay here."

"I can't leave," she said with gentle cheerfulness, even as she nudged the door open and maneuvered her way around him, away from the huge raindrops that had started falling outside. "There's a storm coming and besides, the nice fisherman who brought me over in his powerboat has left already." Her huge tote bag hung from her shoulder and threatened to slip off as she lifted the box she'd brought. "Where do you want me to put these?"

"Where do I want you to…?" Justice repeated in disbelief. "As far away from me as possible. Antarctica would do fine." His voice held a military curtness and a drill inspector loudness.

Kelly didn't flinch but instead allowed his anger and his words to roll off her like water off a duck. "That voice isn't going to work on me, so you might as well save your energy and your vocal cords. You're not going to scare me away."

"Don't be so sure of that, little girl."

Okay, so now his voice held a dangerous edge that did make her a tad nervous. But she couldn't afford to let that show. And she also couldn't afford to let him know how glad she was to see him.

She'd only been thirteen the last time she'd seen him. He'd been marrying her older sister at the time. He'd looked so tall and heroic to her young eyes. He'd adored Barbie and had from the moment he'd met her three years earlier in high school.

Justice and Barbie had gotten married right after graduation. Two years later they'd gotten divorced.

"Why are you here?" Justice demanded. "Haven't you Hart women messed up my life enough already? Have you come to gloat or something? To kick a guy when he's down, is that it?"

Kelly set the heavy box on a nearby table before turning to face him. "I came here to help."

"I don't need your help."

Outside, skeletal veins of lightning flashed and flowed like rivers of light while thunder boomed, rattling the floor-to-ceiling windows in the beach house. Impressive. But the storm didn't hold a candle to the fire in Justice's eyes.

There was something more to his anger, something she couldn't quite put her finger on. Something else reflected in his gaze. Was it bitterness or despair? It was there and gone as fast as a flash of lightning. Maybe she'd imagined that flare of emotion, but there was no way she was ignoring it. "I'm a physical therapist, Justice. I can help you."

"I don't need your help," he repeated, his voice gritty, a muscle in his jaw clenching. "I don't need it and I don't *want* it."

"I know that's what you think right now, but you'll change your mind."

"That's what your sister, Barbie, thought. That she'd change my mind about being a Marine. That she'd change my mind about playing Ken to her Barbie-doll life. It ain't gonna happen," Justice drawled.

Score one for the Marine. Kelly was stung by the comparison to her sister. She and Barbie had little in common. Her older sister liked being surrounded by adoring men and needed love and plenty of male attention to feel fulfilled. Barbie wasn't a bad person, she just had different priorities from Kelly's.

At the moment, Kelly's priority was dealing with Justice.

She busied herself opening the box. "I brought food. I wasn't sure how many provisions you had here, so I thought it was better to be safe than sorry.''

"If you really thought that, then you'd never have come here in the first place.''

"You've got me there," Kelly admitted with a grin. "So I don't always play it safe, I admit it. Ah, I see the kitchen.'' She made a beeline for it, bringing the box of food with her and leaving Justice to follow her.

She surreptitiously noted his awkward movement. He was still limping, but his mother had told Kelly that the doctors said that was due to the serious bruising and cuts on his leg. He also suffered a slight concussion. But it was his right arm and shoulder that were the real problem.

"What do you think you're doing?'' He had to raise his voice to be heard over the increasing thunder, in addition to the banging of pots and pans as she searched for what she wanted.

"Making dinner," Kelly replied. "I don't know about you, but I haven't eaten since I had a burger along the interstate down from Nashville.''

Justice was tempted to ask her what she was doing in Nashville, but he refused to give her the satisfaction of showing any curiosity about her.

His ex-wife's little sister had certainly grown up. She was wearing baggy cargo pants with flowers on the knees and a lime-green cropped T-shirt that showed the pale skin along the small of her back as she bent over to return the pile of pots to the cabinet. Her wavy, light-brown hair was gathered into a single braid held in place by some sort of flower twisty-thing. She wasn't wearing any jewelry aside from a sensible watch and silly dangle earrings shaped like question marks.

Justice certainly had plenty of questions. "How did you know where I was?"

"Your mother told me," Kelly replied. "She's worried about you."

"Why would my mother tell my ex-wife's sister she was worried about me?"

"Ask her."

"I'm asking you."

"And I prefer that you ask her. You should call her, anyway, to let her know you're okay."

"She has no cause to be worried about me," he said gruffly.

"Right," she noted with a wry smile in his direction. "I can't imagine why she was the teeniest bit concerned that her oldest son took off from the hospital against doctor's orders to hide out on a practically deserted coastal island."

"I am *not* hiding out," he said in a gritty voice. "A Marine does not hide out."

"Hey, fella, I'll have you know that you're not the first Marine I've treated," she informed him before setting a saucepan on the stove and pouring in a batch of homemade soup from a plastic container she'd brought with her. "I know all about the Marine's set of values. Honor, courage, commitment. Not stupidity, however. I saw no reference to stupidity."

Justice couldn't believe the way she'd barged into his domain and made herself at home. He was a member of the Marine Corps' elite Force Recon, the best of the best. He could take out an enemy sniper before they knew what hit them.

Or he used to be able to do that. The docs had warned him that those days were gone now.

Justice couldn't believe it—years of living on the

edge, of making danger his friend, and he got hurt not on a mission but by driving in the States on a normal sunny day.

And now they hailed him as a hero. If they only knew....

The inner torment streaked through him, overshadowing the physical pain he'd been living with since the accident. Gritting his teeth, he battened down his emotions and blocked out the raw fear and guilty doubts that plagued him.

Lightning flashed overhead and thunder crashed a second later. Kelly didn't even flinch as she added salt to the soup.

Her calmness irritated him even further.

His life was in a mess, and she was cooking soup.

Yeah, she might have grown up, but she was still as much a nuisance as ever. And he wasn't about to let her into his life. No matter how good that darn soup was starting to smell.

First thing in the morning he would send her packing. But first he'd eat. He needed food to regain his strength, and there was no contest that what she was cooking had to be better than the stuff he'd been eating lately.

But she wasn't staying. No way. He'd have her off-island on tomorrow's every-other-day ferry to the mainland.

"So what's the deal with you and my mother?" he demanded, carefully lowering himself into a straight-backed kitchen chair.

Kelly looked guilty. His eyes narrowed. Something was up here.

Kelly tried sidestepping the issue once again by repeating her earlier mantra. "Maybe you should ask her."

"I'm asking you," he said, grimacing as he removed the sling in order to use his right hand. He couldn't afford to keep babying it. This was his shooting arm. He had to regain his mobility ASAP. Regardless of what the doctors said.

She placed a huge bowl of soup in front of him along with a few thick slices of what looked like homemade bread. "And I'm saying you should ask your mother. You have a cell phone with you, right? So you can call her and let her know you're all right."

"Why this sudden concern?"

"It's not sudden," she denied, putting her own bowl of soup on the table across from him.

"So you've been pining for me all these years?" he mocked, and was surprised by the flash of something in her eyes. Such big brown eyes for such a little thing. Well, maybe not such a little thing, he silently revised, remembering how the top of her head had brushed his chin as she'd slipped past him to get into the house.

"Yeah, I've been positively lovesick for years," she mocked right back, even going so far as to bat her eyelashes at him with such outrageous excess that he would have smiled…if he'd been a smiling man. But he wasn't.

He focused his attention on the soup. It was good. It wasn't until he saw the satisfied grin on her face that he realized he'd just guzzled down his chow like a raw recruit at boot camp. He dropped his spoon so abruptly it clattered on the wooden table.

"Don't get too comfy here," he warned her. "You're leaving first thing in the morning."

His pronouncement was accentuated by a crack of thunder.

"Sounds like a doozy of a storm," she noted a second before the lights flickered and went out. "Good thing I'm not afraid of the dark," she calmly added. "How about you?"

"I'm a Marine. I live for the dark."

That didn't surprise Kelly. She'd sensed the darkness in him from the moment he'd opened the door. There was a new edge to him, a sharper dangerous edge that hadn't been there before. Brought about by his years in the Marines or by his accident? Or a combination of both?

She could hear him breathing. There was something surprisingly sensual about being caught in the darkness with him, surrounded by velvety shadows illuminated by flashes of lightning. The harsh bursts of light captured the angles of his face, lending them new definition. It was the face of a man who wouldn't step aside if trouble got in his way.

She reached for his empty bowl only to have her fingers collide with his. Heat shot through her, as powerful as a lightning strike. The storm outside dimmed as her senses shifted to the storm raging inside of her body. She could feel the excitement burning in her like a wild thing.

"There's something I should warn you about this beach house," Justice said, his voice silky soft. "There's only one bed."

Chapter Two

"Only one bed, huh?" Kelly frantically tried to hide the fact that her heart had just kicked into overdrive. She couldn't afford to let Justice know that he was getting to her. That wouldn't do at all.

For one thing, Justice clearly didn't think of her that way. He viewed her as a nuisance. For another, she couldn't get involved with him. He was a patient. Or about to become one. Not to mention that he was her sister's ex-husband. A definite hornet's nest there. Way too much baggage.

The lights came back on, and as they did, Kelly knew what she had to do. She had to be sensible here. She also had to keep her sense of humor. It had gotten her through in the past whenever things were tough.

With that in mind, she gave Justice a deliberately mocking look. "Well, I suppose I could arm wrestle you for the bed, but as it happens I brought a sleeping bag with me. And I noticed that your couch in the living room looked pretty comfy."

"Comfy? Do not get comfy here," Justice warned her. "You will not be staying."

His irritated words rolled right off her back. She had her "sensible" coating on now, and nothing he could say should get to her now. The realization comforted her. So did the fact that her smile threw him as she patted his left, uninjured arm. "You know, it's a good thing I'm not the sensitive kind or I'd be hurt by your eagerness to get rid of me. I know, however, what's behind it."

He gave her one of those aggravated looks men give women they don't understand. "I'll tell you what's behind it, the fact that I want you out of here."

"So you've said. We'll talk about it in the morning, if you'd rather." She started cleaning up after their meal, taking their dirty bowls to the kitchen sink and running the water.

"I'd *rather* you were gone."

Thunder boomed one final time, rattling the windowpanes with its bass reverberations. Despite the rumblings, the storm was actually weakening. Just like Justice. He was rumbling like the thunder, but it was more bark than bite. "You're starting to sound like a broken record, Justice."

"I can't figure out why you'd want to stay somewhere you're not wanted."

"Besides being a glutton for punishment, you mean?" She squirted dishwashing liquid into the sink. There was a dishwasher, but she felt the need to scrub. "I've already told you, your mother asked me to come check on you."

"So now you've checked. I'm still alive."

"Have you called her on your cell phone yet?"

"What are you, my keeper?" His voice was really irritated now.

She turned to face him directly as she issued her challenge. "I thought Marines didn't need keepers."

He automatically straightened. "We don't."

"Then act like it, and call your mother."

Justice looked like he wanted to strangle her, before he pivoted and marched out of the room to what she presumed was the only bedroom. The fact that he didn't slam the door but instead closed it with controlled precision didn't fool her for one second. The man was furious with her.

Kelly paused in her nervous tidying to sink onto a nearby kitchen chair. Okay, so maybe Justice wasn't weakening like the departing storm. Maybe she'd been a little overconfident thinking she had things under control.

Only one bed…

His words kept replaying in her mind as she quickly took stock of her surroundings. The living room she'd walked through had a gorgeous pine floor but little furniture aside from the neutral-colored couch. The kitchen was equally no-frill. There was no particular color scheme, the walls were white as was the woodwork. The bathroom was at the end of the hallway, right next to the bedroom with its one bed.

She could easily picture Justice on that bed, his lean fighter's body tangled in satin sheets….

Rats. Only in the beach house for an hour and already she was having sexual fantasies about Justice. Not good.

Time to remind herself yet again why she was here. Because of Mrs. Wilder. Kelly would do anything for the older woman, including walking over fire. And it looked like dealing with Justice would come darn close to that fiery fate.

Kelly would manage. It's what she did best. Her older sister, Barbie, looked gorgeous and Kelly...well, Kelly managed. Barbie brought men to their knees in adoration and Kelly managed not to care that she faded into the wallpaper whenever her sister was around.

"It's a good thing you're so smart," their father had often told Kelly when she was growing up. "Because you're not as beautiful as your sister, so you need something else to make things balance out."

But things had never felt balanced to Kelly. Growing up, she'd often felt like a forgotten member of the family. Her mother, a beauty like Barbie, had referred to Kelly as her "foundling child" because she hadn't inherited their blond-and-blue-eyed coloring and instead had taken after her father with brown hair and eyes.

When her mother died in an automobile accident, Kelly had been devastated. She'd despaired of ever being anything but the gangly, awkward thirteen-year-old she was, of ever showing her mother that she *was* her daughter and did belong.

And there was no depending on her sister during that time, because Barbie had spent every moment with Justice, accepting his marriage proposal only a few weeks after their mother's death.

Justice and Barbie had been going together throughout high school, but even so, Kelly was surprised that Barbie had agreed to marry Justice. He'd already signed up to join the Marines after graduation. Barbie had told her that she was off to live an adventurous life.

Which left Kelly alone with her father, who tried unsuccessfully to hide how much he missed his wife and oldest daughter. He was proud of Kelly's good grades and bragged about how smart she was, but he and Kelly never shared the special bond that he had with Barbie.

Mrs. Wilder had been a lifesaver during those difficult times, stepping into a maternal role with ease. Ever since then they'd continued to share a special bond, despite the divorce between Barbie and Justice.

Yes, Kelly would do anything for Mrs. Wilder. Even face a lion like Justice in his den.

She wondered if he knew that Barbie had recently gotten engaged to a wealthy Atlanta businessman? If so, did that knowledge contribute to his bad mood, to his coming to this island? He'd certainly still sounded bitter when he'd said, *Haven't you Hart women messed up my life enough already?*

Kelly had anticipated that Justice might be angry at her sudden appearance, but she hadn't expected her own response to him. Sure she'd had a teenage crush on him, but that had been ages ago. There hadn't been any way for her to foresee the powerful physical effect he had on her now. And she'd only just arrived. There was bound to be more touching the more time she spent with him.

If she became his physical therapist, they'd be in close physical contact. She had to be prepared for that. But the one thing she wasn't prepared to do was fall in love with Justice Wilder.

Justice was *not* having a good evening. He wasn't getting any more information out of his mother than he'd gotten out of Kelly.

"You forget, Justice, I've been interrogated by the best—your father. You're not going to get me to tell you anything I choose not to," his mom told him. "It didn't work when you were ten and trying to find out what I got you for your birthday and it's not going to work now."

"I'm injured, you shouldn't be picking on me."

"That's right, you're injured and you shouldn't be giving me white hair by taking off from the hospital against doctor's orders."

So much for trying the sympathy routine. "I'm fine," he said impatiently.

"We both know that's not true." His mother's voice was quiet but firm. She'd never been one to take any guff. As the only female in a household of five men—her husband and four strapping sons—she couldn't afford to be a pushover.

"So you sent little Kelly here to take care of me?"

"She's good at what she does, Justice. Let her help you."

"I don't need any help."

"You can always tell a Marine, but you can't tell them much," she muttered before growling, "Don't be such an idiot."

"Gee, thanks, Mom."

"I mean it, Justice." She was using her sternest

voice. "You be nice to Kelly. I sent her there. It wasn't her idea to go."

"I'm a grown man, I don't need my mother sending anyone to help me. I've faced plenty of danger on my own."

"I know that," she said quietly. "And I know the nickname you earned in your squad because of it. Invincible. Able to do the impossible. It's almost as if you were tempting the fates to do something to you. If there was a dangerous mission, you were on it."

"It's what I do." Or what he *used* to do. Who knew what his future held now? He glared down at his injured shoulder and tried to ball his right hand into a fist and raise his arm. It was a pitiful effort.

"And worrying about you and taking care of you is what I do," his mother countered. "I've let you do your job all these years, now let me do mine. Just give physical therapy a try with Kelly and see how things turn out."

"I don't want her here."

"You can't throw her out." His mother sounded panicked, which made him feel guilty.

"I won't throw her out," he said gruffly. "It's storming outside." Lightning flashed again. "I wouldn't turn a dog out in this kind of weather."

"How kind of you to liken Kelly to a dog," she noted wryly.

"Okay, so I don't have my brother's charming ways with women," Justice retorted.

"I'm not asking you to be charming, just to be nice. Think you can do that? I'm only nagging you because I love you."

His throat suddenly clenched. "I know that. Listen, I've got to go, Mom. I only called you to let you know I'm okay.''

He quickly ended the call and tossed his cell phone onto the night table. He'd lied to his mom. He wouldn't be okay until he'd recovered. He was Invincible once. He needed to be Invincible again. Or die trying.

''My mom told me to be nice to you,'' Justice drawled a few minutes later as he watched Kelly wipe down the stove.

''And you told her you've been the perfect host, right?'' she drawled right back.

''I told her I wouldn't toss you out on your keister in a storm.'' A boom of thunder crashed as if to emphasize his statement. Noting her startled jump, he said, ''Are you afraid?''

She tossed the sponge back into the sink before turning to face him again. ''Sorry to disappoint you, but no, I'm not afraid of storms. Actually I think they're kind of neat. And pretty amazing. Did you know that lightning bolts are rarely thicker than a common pencil?''

''You're just a fountain of information, aren't you?''

''I'm a smart woman.''

''Not smart enough to stay away from me.''

She sighed. ''What is it going to take to convince you that I can help you?''

''A miracle?''

''How about a game of poker?''

He narrowed his blue eyes. ''You're kidding, right?''

"If I beat you, then you'll stop being such a baby about my being your physical therapist."

Justice stared at her in amazement. Did she have any idea who she was speaking to here? He was a member of the Marine Corps' most elite Force Recon. He knew twenty ways to disable an enemy in the blink of an eye. He'd used deadly force. And she was calling him a baby and challenging him to a poker game? She clearly wasn't as smart as she claimed to be.

"What happens when I win?" he countered.

"Then I'll leave on the next ferry."

He found that hard to believe. Not when she'd been so adamant about staying. She didn't appear to be the type to give up easily if at all. Stubborn. Just like his ex-wife. Definitely another troublemaking Hart woman—the last thing he needed in his life. "What's the catch?" he demanded.

"No catch. I happen to have a deck of cards with me."

"I'm sure you do." He didn't trust her for one minute. The woman was up to something. Whatever it was, he wasn't about to let her get away with it. "And I'm sure you won't mind if I examine them first."

"Afraid I'm going to cheat the big bad Marine?"

"It wouldn't surprise me if you tried. After all, you are Barbie's sister."

"I'm nothing like my sister."

"No, you're not, are you."

His comment stung for some reason. Maybe it was the way he was looking at her, as if dismissing her.

Okay, so she wasn't gorgeous like Barbie. That

didn't mean she didn't have other redeeming characteristics.

Like being smart? an inner voice mocked.

Like being strong, she silently countered. And making the most of what she had. And being independent. Unlike Barbie, she didn't need outside reinforcement to feel complete. She didn't need constant reassurance and male adoration.

Kelly narrowed her eyes at him, giving him a don't-mess-with-me look. "No, I'm not my sister. I'm something even better."

"Really. And what's that?"

"A woman not to be trifled with."

He raised one dark eyebrow. "Trifled with, huh? I'll keep that in mind."

"You do that." She walked over to her backpack and reached into an outside pocket. "Here are the cards." She handed them to him. "Check them out. Then prepare for a trouncing."

"First trifle now trouncing." His voice was mocking.

So was hers. "What's wrong, is my vocabulary too big for you?"

"I'll try and keep up."

"I hope it isn't too much of a strain for you."

"I think I can handle it." *And you.* The look he gave her made that much clear.

She'd forgotten how blue his eyes were. It was like being bathed in the deep ocean, his gaze washing over her.

"We'll have to see," she replied, backing away from him…and temptation.

"Want me to deal?"

"No, I'll deal. I feel it only fair to warn you that

when I play cards with my nursing buddies, I often end up winning.''

"I'm shaking in my boots.''

Actually he was barefoot. He had nicely formed feet leading up to muscular calves and thighs. Don't go there, she sternly warned herself, tearing her gaze away.

"I feel it only fair to warn you that when I play cards with my Force Recon buddies, I *always* win," Justice said.

"Then we've both been warned." She sat down at the table where they'd recently eaten and waited patiently for Justice to join her before adding, "May the best woman win."

Kelly didn't feel one iota of guilt for not informing him of the summer she spent working at an Atlantic City casino and learning card tricks from a seventy-year-old gentleman gambler named Diamond Mick. She deliberately dealt the cards a tad awkwardly, not like a complete novice but not like one confident of winning. She didn't want to overplay her hand here. Let Justice think she was a bit nervous.

The truth was she never cheated when playing gin rummy with her nursing buddies. But poker was another thing. She rarely got the chance to practice what Diamond Mick had taught her, other than practicing in front of a mirror to make sure she hadn't lost her touch.

They only played one hand. As it turned out she didn't have to cheat, she was dealt a fantastic set.

The problem was that Justice looked equally thrilled with whatever he had. What if *he* cheated?

She'd have to count on a Marine's code of honor

preventing him from doing that. Maybe his confidence was his way of trying to bluff her into folding. That wasn't going to happen.

She called his bet. Justice set down his cards, spreading them out with a confident grin. "Read 'em and weep. Four of a kind."

"Very impressive. But I believe a straight flush beats four of a kind every time." And she set down her own cards.

"I don't believe this."

"I didn't cheat."

"I know you didn't, I was watching you like a hawk."

Kelly was relieved that she hadn't had to practice her card trick skills after all. She'd forgotten that as a Force Recon Marine, Justice had unusually acute powers of observation.

"So we're agreed. I stay on as your physical therapist. Good." Kelly didn't even wait for him to reply. "That's all settled, then. Well, it's getting late and I've had a full day. I think I'll turn in."

"Go right ahead." His look dared her to get ready for bed in front of him.

She had no such qualms. Once her sleeping bag was comfortably arranged on the couch, she tugged on a huge sleepshirt over her head and upper torso. Under cover of the thick cotton material she expertly wiggled and maneuvered her T-shirt and bra right off, tugging them out the armhole and into her backpack in one deft operation.

Justice appeared stunned by her behavior. Good. She liked to keep him on his toes. She was not about to retreat into the bathroom to get ready for bed like some shy miss. She could adopt as much of a don't-mess-with-me stance as any Marine. It was all about attitude with a capital *A*.

"Where'd you learn to do that?" Justice asked.

"My co-ed college dorm. Were you suitably impressed?"

"Were you trying to impress me?"

She shook her head.

"Good." His voice was curt. "Because I don't need you going all goofy over me like you did as a teenager."

Kelly wanted to disappear into the floorboards. She hadn't realized he'd noticed her crush. He'd never said anything at the time. Probably because he'd been too nice. He wasn't nice any longer. That much was clear.

She couldn't let him know he'd bothered her. Tucking her "sensible" facade around her once more, she managed a brilliant smile. "Jeez, Justice, that was ages ago. Get over yourself, would you? The bottom line is that you can relax because overbearing Marines aren't my type," she assured him. "I promise not to go all goofy over you. Don't worry, you're safe with me."

The question was, would she be safe with him?

Chapter Three

The kiss was divine. A warm masculine mouth tenderly parted her lips. Hands slipped over her willing body, caressing her with skill and passion. The moment had come. The waiting was over. This was it...

"Rise and shine!" a voice boomed over Kelly's head.

Startled, she jerked awake and almost ended up rolling right off the couch in her sleeping bag.

"Hold on there." Justice grabbed her with his good hand.

She'd been dreaming. Blinking rapidly, Kelly tried to take stock of her surroundings. But her immediate attention was focused on Justice.

He'd caught her, preventing her fall with his body. He was so close to her she could feel the warmth of his lean body, could almost hear his heartbeat. She could certainly feel her own heart beating wildly.

She could also feel every one of his fingers. He

wasn't holding her that tightly. She was just super-sensitized to his touch, deliciously rough against her soft skin. He had calluses. He smelled of soap and shaving cream. She was wildly tempted to sniff his cheek, to lean closer and fall into his incredibly blue eyes....

"Hey," he said gruffly, "I thought you promised that you weren't going to throw yourself at my feet."

A bucket of cold water couldn't have snapped her out of her momentary reverie faster. "I'd like to throw something, all right," she muttered, shifting away from him on the couch. "And not at your feet. At your head. What time is it?"

"O-five hundred."

"Five in the morning?" She hadn't gotten to sleep until after one, tossing and turning on the couch. And that dream she was having was just getting really good. Not that she'd been dreaming about Justice. She hadn't. She was sure that the man in her dreams bore a striking resemblance to the sexy actor Dylan McDermott. That was her story and she was sticking to it.

"Affirmative. Time to rise and shine and get this physical therapy thing going," Justice stated. "The faster we get started, the faster we'll be done, and then you can go your way and I can return to my tour of duty."

"First I need to see your medical records."

"I've got them here." Using his left hand, he waved them in front of her sleepy face. "Had them faxed from the mainland."

"Fine. I'll read them." She barely stifled a yawn. "But first I need coffee and a shower, in that order."

"Go ahead, but be fast about it. No dawdling for an hour in the bathroom trying to make yourself beautiful."

"I could stay in the bathroom for a week and I still wouldn't be beautiful," she wryly retorted. "I told you, I'm not my sister."

"So I'm learning."

"Oh, so you are capable of learning? That's an encouraging sign."

"You sure are a feisty little thing, aren't you."

She rolled her eyes. "Oh puhlease! For one thing, I'm not little. I'm five foot seven in my bare feet. For another I'm not feisty."

"Could have fooled me."

"Yes, but then you're a Marine, easy to fool."

"You're just saying that to get to me," Justice calmly replied. "See? I am learning."

"Yes, you are. And you're blocking my way to my morning caffeine so move, or face my wrath."

"Wrath, huh? Is that anything like trifling with a trouncing?"

"No, it's much worse. Now move."

"Not a morning person, are we?" At her fiery look, he backed up. "Okay, okay, I'm moving."

Still bleary-eyed, she headed for the kitchen and the thermos of coffee she'd left there last night. Cold coffee was better than no coffee. It was actually still a little warm, and she felt the caffeine hit her system as she grabbed clean clothes from her backpack on her way to the bathroom.

A shower helped restore her. She dressed quickly, pulling on a pair of shorts and a T-shirt. Her hair was still damp as she returned to the kitchen to confront Justice.

Only now did she notice the shirt he was wearing, which was one of those brilliant multicolored Hawaiian designs. How could she have missed that before? "Nice shirt," she noted.

"It's not mine," he growled. "My buddy Striker owns this beach house and a collection of gaudy Hawaiian shirts."

Judging from Justice's disgusted expression, she figured he hadn't chosen to borrow his friend's clothes out of a desire to make a fashion statement. No doubt his injury made getting in and out of a button-down shirt easier than a T-shirt like he'd been wearing last night. And no doubt Justice hadn't brought any shirts of his own, or he'd be wearing them and not this tropical number. He hadn't done up all the buttons, leaving a sexy amount of his chest bare.

Time to change the subject, she decided. "So what's for breakfast?"

"Toasted physical therapists," he drawled.

Kelly cracked up. "I don't believe it. The brooding Justice Wilder actually made a joke. This has got to be a first."

"Who said it was a joke?"

"I'm tougher than I look. You don't want to dine on me, believe me." She opened the fridge and pulled out the fresh eggs in the box of provisions she'd brought with her yesterday. "How do scrambled eggs sound?"

His growling stomach was answer enough. Hers quickly followed suit. "Okay." She reached for a frying pan. "A big rasher of scrambled eggs coming right up."

Justice surreptitiously watched her as she moved

around the kitchen with a speedy efficiency. She was
into multitasking—beating the eggs with a fork in
one hand while she popped pieces of bread into the
toaster with the other. She seemed to have recovered
from her earlier grouchiness.

Today she was wearing a pair of khaki walking
shorts and a plain pink T-shirt. The sandals she wore
displayed her feet and the neon pink nail polish on
her toenails. Her question mark earrings once again
dangled in her ears. Her damp hair was gathered up
in one of those plastic clip things to keep it out of
her way. She didn't look particularly gorgeous but
he couldn't seem to keep his eyes off her.

Maybe it was her can-do attitude, or her off-key
humming of a Faith Hill country song. She wasn't
her sister. She hadn't spent a lot of time in the bathroom messing with makeup. In fact, he doubted she
was wearing any. But as she passed by his seat at
the small dining table, he noted that she smelled
really good. Not all perfumy, but fresh and sexy.

Sexy? Dismiss that thought. This was his ex-
wife's baby sister here. Okay, so she was only five
years younger than Barbie, which also made her five
years younger than he was. Not a big deal. Age
wasn't the issue here. Family connections were.

She was here for one purpose, or so she said. To
increase his chances of recovering the full use of his
right arm. His shooting arm. He'd been one of the
best sharpshooters Force Recon had ever seen. And
now he sat here barely able to pick up a damn cup
of coffee.

"What makes you think you can do anything to
help me recover the mobility in my arm?" he
abruptly demanded.

"The fact that I'm good at what I do. But I need to review your medical records before I can tell you anything definite, read the doctor's orders for your treatment."

"It's all right here." He impatiently shoved the file across the table, wanting those incriminating papers away from him. He already knew what they said by heart. Prognosis: unknown. Critical ligament damage...full recovery of mobility unlikely.

Well, Justice had dealt with "unlikely" and "unknown" before. More times than he could count, in fact. It had been unlikely that he would survive that last mission in a certain Middle Eastern country rumored to harbor terrorists.

But he had survived. Only to come back to the States to get injured.

"I forgot to ask you last night, how does it feel to be hailed a hero for rescuing that little boy from that burning car?" She placed a plate of fluffy scrambled eggs in front of him.

"It stinks."

"Hey, I'm not that bad a cook," she protested. "So I overcooked the eggs a little."

"I meant that stupid hero thing. It's not true."

"It's not true that you rescued a toddler from the back seat of a burning car after you witnessed a car accident near Camp Lejeune?"

"I don't want to talk about it," Justice growled.

"Fine." She shrugged and sat down across from him, digging into her own breakfast. "We can discuss something else. Like how much you love my gourmet cooking."

"The eggs are good," he grudgingly admitted.

"Oh, my! I do declare that such flowery praise

will surely go to my head.'' She dramatically placed the back of her hand across her forehead in the manner of a swooning Southern miss.

Instead of acknowledging her mocking comment, he said, ''How long will it take you to review my medical records?''

''Not long. I'm a fast reader.''

''Good. Because I want to get started on this op as soon as possible.''

''Op?''

''This operation, this mission.''

''I see. So you're considering your recovery as you would any mission assigned to you? That's a good thing, I suppose.''

''A Marine never fails.''

''We both know that's not true.''

''If you're referring to my failed marriage to your sister—''

''I wasn't,'' she quickly interrupted him. ''I meant that no one can guarantee a 100 percent success rate at anything.''

''No excuses, no exceptions.''

''Seems like a pretty tough philosophy to maintain.''

''The Marine Corps is supposed to be tough. It's not a place for wimps.''

''Yeah, physical therapy is like that. Not a place for wimps. Oh, I almost forgot…'' She returned to the counter to hand him the special concoction she'd mixed up in the blender. It did not escape his notice that she'd only poured one glass, not two. One glass, just for him. ''Here, drink this.''

He grabbed her wrist. ''What did you put in here?''

Startled, she tried to pull away.

"Answer me. What did you put in here?"

"Wheat germ, a banana, some strawberries, orange juice, a little vitamin B."

"And what else?"

"Nothing else."

"Do you swear on my mother's life?"

His expression made her shiver. "Yes."

He abruptly released her wrist.

"Why?" Her voice was husky with emotion. "What did you think I'd put in there?"

"My pain medication."

She stared at him in amazement. "You thought I was trying to drug you against your will?"

"That thought did cross my mind, yes."

"You clearly have a suspicious mind."

"It's kept me alive more times than I can count."

"We're not in a battle zone here."

"Doesn't matter. It's an ingrained part of my training, thinking of scenarios and outcomes, thinking of everything as a weapon, even this fork." He used the utensil to eat the last bite of scrambled eggs. "You call it being suspicious, I call it being alert, never letting down my defenses."

She realized then how deep his distrust truly ran—not just of her but of everyone and everything around him.

"If I gave you my word that I won't drug you, that it's completely unethical for me to do so, would that make you feel better? If I swore on your mother's life, as you put it, would that make you feel better?"

"The only thing that will make me feel better is regaining complete mobility of my arm and rejoining my squadron. Anything less than that is unacceptable.''

Kelly had worked with patients before who'd been unable to accept their injuries and the limitations that had subsequently been placed on them. Inevitably it made their recoveries slower. But there was no speeding up the acceptance process. Each individual had to get there at their own rate, in their own time, in their own way. She had a feeling that Justice's way would be the hard way. He wasn't a man to take the easy route.

She didn't even realize that she was absently rubbing her wrist until he spoke.

''I'm sorry if I hurt you.''

''I'm sorry you didn't trust me,'' she replied. ''That's bound to make this process more difficult.''

''I told you, I don't trust anyone.''

''Not even your own family?''

''Of course I trust them.''

''Then trust that your mother knew what she was doing when she sent me to you.''

''I trust her, not her judgment about everything.''

''Oh, so you think I conned your mother into sending me here?'' Kelly asked mockingly. ''Sure, I can understand that. After all, she's such a gullible lady. Very naive. Easy to fool. Nothing to pull the wool over her eyes. An easy mark. A real bubblehead.''

''Hey, nobody calls my mom a bubblehead,'' Justice growled.

''My point exactly. She's one of the sharpest women I've ever met.''

''Okay, okay, so my mother is not easily fooled. Point taken.''

"I hope so. I'd rather not have this conversation every time I offer you a drink. Think of all the energy you're expending on that distrust."

"It's not wasted energy."

"Yes, it is. That mind-set may be useful during one of your covert special ops, as you called them, but you don't need that kind of defense mechanism in this situation. You're safe here."

Didn't she understand that he wasn't safe anywhere? He'd let down his guard when he'd rushed in to save that toddler, and look where it had gotten him. If he'd been more alert, he might have fallen differently. He'd been trained to drop and roll and had avoided injury so many times in the past. It was one of the reasons he'd gotten his nickname.

No, he definitely was not safe, not from the nightmares about the car bursting into flames, not about the doubts that he refused to even acknowledge.

He had no room in his life for such things.

Kelly claimed she could help him, fine. Here was her chance to prove it. He'd always been a man who believed more in actions than words.

That didn't mean he trusted Kelly, or her motives. Bottom line was that she was still his ex-wife's sister and his divorce had not exactly been an amicable one. Kelly might still have some sort of hidden agenda for coming here. Which meant he'd have one, too.

Point, counterpoint, strike, counterstrike. It's what he did, how he thought. Trust was not a requirement for getting the use of his arm back.

"You'd better start reviewing my medical report so we can get this op under way." He impatiently waited while she read through the file. "Well?

What's the plan? You do have a plan, right?''

"Give me a minute here."

"Because planning plays as important a role in the preparation of battle as in the conduct of battle."

"Which is all very well and good but we're not talking about a battle here."

"Yes, we are. I'm not stupid enough to think otherwise. It's going to be a battle to get my strength back."

"There's no guarantee your arm will recover fully, but you have a much better chance of increasing your range of mobility with physical therapy and time."

"I don't have much time and I'm not interested in merely increasing my range of mobility. I want my arm back the way it was before."

"I can't guarantee that will happen, Justice," she said quietly.

"No excuses, no exceptions."

"And no false promises of a miracle cure. We can just take this one step at a time and see how things progress. Deal?"

She held out her hand.

He reluctantly took it in his. His fingers were warm against her skin as he gingerly wrapped them around her hand. Even something as simple as a handshake proved difficult. Gritting his teeth, he silently railed against his own weakness.

"Don't push yourself to do too much too soon, that will do more damage than good," she warned him.

"Have you always been this bossy?"

"No, I think I've become bossier with age and

now I'm getting pretty darn good at it. Which is a good thing considering that you're used to drill instructors screaming orders at you. But don't worry, I'll try not to be too hard on you. No marching orders, none of that 'right face' or 'forward march' stuff."

"Stuff?"

"Not the appropriate military terminology? Sorry about that. Medical terminology is more my thing. For example, antibodies. Everyone knows that antibodies are against everyone. And that an enema is not a friend. Hey, was that a smile I saw there, soldier?"

"I'm a Marine, not a soldier."

"Sorry, I'll repeat the question. Was that a smile I saw there, Mr. Big Bad Marine?"

"It was gas."

"Listen, buddy, any more jabs at my cooking and you'll be pulling kitchen duty. And don't even think about calling me a feisty little thing again."

"I wasn't going to."

"Good."

"I'm still waiting to hear your plan."

"Okay, then. Here it is. We start out nice and easy..." Kelly began when he immediately interrupted her.

"I don't like that plan."

She gave a long-suffering sigh. "Maybe this should be the part where I point out that I'm the one with the training and you're the one who is supposed to be heeding my advice."

"I don't do nice and easy," Justice informed her.

She was not impressed. "Then it's about time you learned. Just pretend you're back in boot camp."

Now he looked insulted. "There's nothing nice or easy about boot camp. It's twelve weeks of grueling and exhausting work meant to separate the cream of the crop from the rest."

"You didn't let me finish. As I was saying before I was so rudely interrupted, just pretend you're back in boot camp, only this time instead of your goal being to become a Marine, your goal is to increase your mobility. You're very lucky that overall you're in such good physical shape."

"Lucky?"

She noted the bitterness in his voice. "Yes, lucky. I've dealt with patients who have terminal illnesses, patients who have been paralyzed by car accidents. Compared to them, you're sitting pretty."

"You have no idea what you're dealing with here." His curt words were like bullets. "I'm a member of the Marine Corps' most elite force, which means I have to be at the top of my game. I have to pass stringent physical exams to return to my squad. These are men who can drop and do a few hundred one-handed push-ups without even breaking a sweat. My injury may seem measly to you..."

"It's not measly, Justice. I'm sorry if I gave you that impression. The bruising and lacerations on your legs will heal with time. And your concussion was slight, although you should have rested and not been traveling out here. But the damage to your shoulder is very serious indeed. I wasn't trying to belittle your injury or the effect it's had on your life. I'm just saying that in the whole spectrum of things, it could have been much worse. You could have been paralyzed or killed when that car exploded."

Justice didn't tell her how he felt, that he might as well have been killed if his future as a member of Force Recon was gone. She wouldn't understand, she couldn't know how much who he was involved what he did. The definition of invincible was "incapable of being overcome or defeated." That was no longer true. Which left Justice feeling incapable, period.

"I realize that a brush with death makes most people question things in their lives…" Kelly began when he interrupted her again.

"Marines aren't most people. And this certainly wasn't the first time I've had a brush with death."

His words chilled her. She'd known his work as a Marine meant he was exposed to danger, but she'd somehow never considered the fact that he might actually die serving his country.

She had to take a sip of freshly brewed coffee before going on. She steadied her trembling fingers by wrapping them around her coffee mug. "Why do you do it? Why do you put your life at risk?"

"Because my country needs me. It's what I do and what I'm good at doing."

"I know you come from a long line of Marines in your family."

"Affirmative." Now he really sounded like a Marine.

"Have you and your brothers ever worked together?"

"Negative."

"You're the only one in Special Forces, right?"

"Affirmative. I'm in Force Recon."

"I suppose you have one of those nifty nicknames like Flyboy or Ranger or something."

"Flyboy was Joe's nickname and Ranger was my brother Mark's nickname when we were all kids."

"I heard that Mark's new security firm Sovereign Securities is doing very well."

"He has a waiting list of clients."

"You still haven't told me *your* nickname," Kelly reminded him. "Wait a minute, I remember now. It had something to do with a bird..."

"Eagle."

She nodded. "A symbol of freedom."

Justice wasn't about to tell her about his Invincible nickname, resulting from his ability to avoid harm in extremely risky missions. At the moment he couldn't even live up to his old nickname of Eagle. A symbol of freedom. Yeah, right. He couldn't even lift his arm. He was a wounded eagle.

Not that you'd know it by the way Kelly was looking at him with those big brown eyes of hers. He didn't want her thinking of him as some kind of hero. There were plenty of women who thought a man in uniform was sexy, who got off on the danger of his work. He hoped she wasn't one of them.

Last night she'd told him to get over himself and had practically laughed at him when he'd warned her not to go all gooey over him. Overbearing Marines weren't her type, she'd claimed.

And bossy physical therapists weren't his. Especially not when said bossy physical therapist was his ex-wife's sister.

So here was the plan. Put her to the test. See if she could make him whole again. Correction, see if she could restore his arm to its previous mobility. There was no way she could make him whole again. He had too many dark corners in his soul to ever be whole again.

Chapter Four

"**I** hope my sister didn't have anything to do with you doing such dangerous work," Kelly said, interrupting Justice's black thoughts.

Justice frowned at her. "Where did that crazy idea come from?"

She looked away. "I know you were upset after the divorce."

"Upset doesn't come close." A Marine never failed, and the collapse of his marriage marked a huge failure in his eyes. His C.O.—commanding officer—had advised him not to get married until Justice was at least twenty-five. But Justice hadn't listened. It was the last time he'd ignored a suggestion from his C.O.

Sure, after the divorce and after he'd signed up for Force Recon and completed his advanced training, he'd been reckless for a time afterward, almost daring fate. But it wasn't because he hadn't thought life was worth living. It was because only when that life-or-death adrenaline was shooting through his body did he really feel alive. And he'd had something to prove. Maybe he still did.

"I know you loved her very much." Kelly's voice was almost wistful.

"Is that why you came here? Because you think I'm still pining away after your sister?"

She shook her head. "I already told you, I came because your mother asked me to."

"Since when have you and my mother been close buddies?"

"You didn't ask her?"

He wasn't about to admit that he'd asked and his mom hadn't told him. "We didn't talk about it, no."

"She was very kind to me during a time when I really needed it, after my mother died."

"So you're repaying a debt?"

"If that's the way you want to think of it."

"That was a long time ago."

Kelly paused before deciding there was no point in avoiding telling him the truth any longer. At least the truth about her relationship with his mother. She wasn't ready to tell him about Barbie's engagement yet, in case he didn't know about it already. She'd given him the chance to say something when she'd brought up the topic of her sister, asking him if Barbie had had anything to do with him taking such risks.

"Your mother and I have kept in touch over the years," Kelly admitted. "Well, more than just kept in touch. We've become friends."

She caught the brief flash of surprise on his face. Not that he was the kind of man who showed much emotion. He wasn't. But she knew him or felt she did, despite the fact that she hadn't seen him in years. He was still Justice. Tougher, more cynical, more mature. But still Justice.

"Why would the two of you become friends?" he demanded. "And why wouldn't my mom have told me about it?"

"Maybe because she didn't think you'd understand."

"I don't," he said bluntly.

She'd known he wouldn't understand, so there was no reason for her to feel disappointment. Suddenly she didn't feel like talking to him about something as personal as her relationship with his mom. "Do you cook?"

He blinked at her non sequitur. "What?"

"You heard me. Do you cook? Because I didn't come here to be your housekeeper. I thought we could share the cooking duties."

"You did, did you?"

"Yes, I did." She gave him a direct look. "You can start with dinner tonight. Do you have a problem with that?"

"I have a problem with a lot of things."

"I noticed that when I first arrived. You weren't exactly in the best of moods."

"Moods?" he said the word as if it were something distasteful. "Moods have nothing to do with it. You chose to come here and walk into the proverbial lion's den."

"I thought your nickname was Eagle, not Lion."

His expression darkened. "Can we forgo the chit-chat and get things moving here? You claimed you could help my recovery, but I have yet to see any proof of that."

"And you're not a man to go on blind faith are you?"

"Not when it involves a Hart woman, no." He held up his hand, stalling her immediate protest. "I know, I know, you're not like your sister. Or so you say. I'll need proof."

"And how am I supposed to prove that? I would have thought my appearance alone would make that point clear." She waved a hand toward her face and then her body.

"There's nothing wrong with your appearance."

"I didn't say there was. But I don't even look anything like Barbie. She's blond and beautiful and I'm not. But enough about that," Kelly said abruptly, feeling uncomfortable comparing herself to her sister yet again. It was not a habit she wanted to fall into with him. "Let's get started with your therapy."

"Remember, I don't do nice and easy," Justice warned her.

"I'll keep that in mind." As if she'd forget there was nothing nice or easy about this job. And that's what it was, the way she had to think of it—a job.

Kelly couldn't rid herself of the sinking feeling it might already be too late for that already, though.

Three hours later Kelly was exhausted. She'd put Justice through a series of range-of-motion exercises. He hadn't liked any of them.

"What kind of wimpy exercise is called a wand exercise?" he'd scoffed.

"Do you want me to rename it the torture exercise?" she retorted.

He ignored her comment and kept ranting. "And

shoulder ladder? Tracing my fingers up the wall?
Another wimpy waste of time.''

She knew his frustration came from his inability
to complete that last exercise because of the weakness of his arm. She also knew weakness had to be
a Marine's deadliest enemy.

Kelly showed Justice some isometric exercises he
could do on his own and left him to it, realizing that
he needed some time alone.

After making herself a tall cold glass of iced tea,
Kelly headed outside onto the large deck facing the
ocean. The white plastic resin chair was warm
against her back and thighs from the sun. She'd
grabbed a bottle of sunscreen, even though it was
now later in the afternoon, and the chance of burning
wasn't as high as it might have been at noon. But
at the moment she was too engrossed in the scenery
to apply the lotion.

How hypnotic the waves were—the sound of
them, the look of them. Watching the combined
forces of nature, the land and the sea tussling together, reminded Kelly of Justice and her. He was
the immovable land and she was the constant ocean.
The recurring power of water was able to wear down
the toughest of land masses. That thought made her
grin for some reason.

The beach in front of her was wide and flat with
finely packed sand. Aside from a medium-large dog
frolicking in the distance, there wasn't another soul
in sight. She had to admit that there was something
rather soothing in being away from the city and sitting there communing with nature.

Sunlight sparkled off the water, creating a shim-
mering-diamond effect. Kelly wasn't sure how long

she sat there before she was interrupted by the arrival of the dog.

"Hi, there," she greeted the animal as it clomped onto the deck and dropped down beside her as if he belonged there. "Where do you live?"

The dog tilted his head toward the house as if in answer to her question.

A moment later Justice opened the door leading to the deck and came outside to join her. "Nice dog you've got," Kelly said.

"I don't have a dog," Justice replied.

"Your friend's dog then."

"He doesn't have a dog, either."

She watched Justice sit on the deck's railing, as if he were a posted lookout. The man never relaxed. If he had a dog, he'd be more relaxed. Not that "relaxed" and "Marine" went together very well. Which brought her back to the dog. "Maybe he belongs to one of your neighbors."

"There are no nearby neighbors, that's why I like it here."

"It is a beautiful place." Kelly returned her attention to the beachscape laid out in front of her. "The Barbary pirates thought so, too. They used the coastal islands off North and South Carolina to hide their ships and their treasure."

"Showing off your fountain of information again, are you?"

"Still in a bad mood again, are you?" she said with a challenging grin.

Their eyes met. She wasn't prepared for the impact. Out here in the sunshine the intensity of his blue eyes was even more apparent. His dark lashes made them even more dramatic. *Even more, even more,* it was a repeating refrain where Justice was concerned.

He was even more attractive than she'd expected, she was even more vulnerable than she'd anticipated.

She wanted him to kiss her even more, even more...

"Hello, there!" someone shouted out, disrupting the moment.

Kelly pulled her gaze from his and looked down the beach, welcoming the interruption. Her thoughts had been getting entirely too tempting, there. Her brain must have been melted by the afternoon sun for her to have even remotely considered the possibility of kissing Justice. That wouldn't do at all.

There were two women approaching. One had short, silver hair, the other long, black hair but both wore jeans and matching T-shirts in a bright green. "It looks like we've got company coming," Kelly noted.

Justice frowned and glared at her accusingly. "Who did you call?"

"No one. What, you think I invited someone over? I don't know anyone on this island."

"Neither do I."

"Well then, I guess that's about to change," she said cheerfully.

"Hello, there," the older woman called out again.

"Hello," Kelly replied, since she was certain that Justice wouldn't make a similar friendly greeting.

"My name is Marge and this is Amelia. We're here about the turtles."

"The turtles?" Being a chocoholic, Kelly's

thoughts immediately turned to the classic choco-
late-covered pecan and caramel candy.

"The sea turtles," Marge clarified. "We're vol-
unteers with the local turtle rescue organization and
since you've only recently come to the island we
wanted to touch base and remind you that May is
the middle of the turtles' nesting season. So we're
asking residents with oceanside property to leave
their lights off at night."

"All the lights?" Kelly still vividly remembered
the intimate shadows created by the darkness last
night when the storm had temporarily knocked out
the electricity.

"Your outside lights," Marge replied. "It's im-
perative that no bright lights appear along the beach
because it affects the sensory devices in the baby
sea turtles as well as the mother. The sea's natural
reflection of light is the only course of movement
their instincts give them. They'll follow the lights
and end up inland where they can become dehy-
drated and die."

Kelly didn't like that picture at all. "I had no
idea."

"Most people don't." Marge smiled as if sensing
Kelly was a kindred spirit. "Loggerhead sea turtles
are older than the dinosaurs and can weigh up to
350 pounds. We have one of the few beaches un-
spoiled enough for them, and we'd like to keep it
that way."

"I can certainly understand why," Kelly agreed.

"During nesting season the females haul themselves out of the surf and pull themselves across the
sand with their huge paddle-like flippers to dig a
nest above the high-tide mark. After she's laid the

eggs, they're covered with sand and then the female moves back to the sea with tears in her eyes."

"Tears," Kelly repeated in amazement. "You mean she's actually crying?"

"Only to keep the sand out of her eyes while she's on the beach," Marge said.

Kelly left her chair to sit on the deck steps, closer to the women. "And what happens to the eggs she's left behind?"

"They're a great delicacy for the raccoons and ghost crabs. That's why our watch group marks a new nest with chicken wire and red flags to protect them from being trampled by humans and being eaten by animals. We also move them by hand, relocating their nest if it's below the tide mark. There is a chain of similar networks all along the East Coast. After surviving a hundred and fifty million years, these turtles are now listed as threatened on the endangered species list because their natural breeding grounds are being taken over by coastal development."

Justice felt like the turtle women had been visiting for two hundred million years. Not because of the information about the plight of the turtle; he actually felt a little sorry for the critters. He knew what it felt like to be like a fish out of water, or in this case a turtle—stranded...unable to return to his natural habitat.

He'd noticed the curious looks the newcomers had given him and his still-scraped-up legs. He'd never been wild about meeting strangers, and since the accident that feeling had certainly increased. He didn't feel like making small talk, he didn't feel like talking period. He had his "war" face on, which was no doubt why the women were giving him a wide berth. They were smarter than Kelly.

"You should keep your dog away from the nests," the younger woman added, speaking for the first time.

"He's not my dog," Justice growled.

As if to prove him a liar, the mutt had the nerve to get up, walk over to Justice, and lie down at his feet to gaze up at him adoringly.

"Do you know who he belongs to?" Kelly asked the women.

They both shook their heads.

"Well, thank you for the warning about our outside lights," Kelly said. "We'll be sure to keep them out at night."

Our lights? Justice couldn't believe she'd just referred to them as *our* lights. There was no *our* here. Next she'd be calling the mutt at his feet *our* dog.

But no, next she had the nerve to invite the turtle women to stay even longer. "Would you ladies like some coffee or iced tea?"

Eyeing Justice's frown a tad nervously, both women wisely refused. Following their gaze, Kelly caught Justice's thunderous expression.

Once they'd left, she told Justice, "That was rude of you."

"I didn't say a word."

"You didn't have to. Your glowering look said it all. And you did say a word. Several of them. You said, 'He's not my dog.'"

"Well, he isn't."

"The dog clearly thinks otherwise."

"I don't care what the aforementioned canine thinks."

"You don't care what most people think, either, do you? I wonder why that is."

Justice didn't like the speculative way Kelly was eyeing him. He didn't need her getting curious about the dark places in his life. "I thought you were a physical therapist, not a psychologist."

"I'm interested in why people react the way they do."

"Well, don't get interested in me," he warned her.

"Of course I'm interested. You're the son of a good friend of mine. You're a patient of mine. As for anything further, I told you last night that there was no chance of that happening. Overbearing Marines still aren't my type. I'm just saying that if you want to talk, I'm willing to listen."

"I've been talking all day."

"I meant talking about your emotions."

He looked as horrified as if she'd just suggested he eat sand. "Force Recon Marines don't have emotions we talk about."

"Makes your life easier that way, does it?"

"Emotions cloud judgment," Justice stated impassively.

She could tell she wasn't going to get any further with him tonight. At least not on that matter. But a tiny part of her couldn't help wondering if he'd have opened up more if she'd been as beautiful as her sister Barbie.

Kelly had read a recent study about female therapists indicating that patients found attractive therapists more competent, effective and trustworthy than those less physically attractive. And while Kelly was merely average in the looks department, she'd noticed that a number of people in her profession looked as if they could have been homecoming queens in high school...like Barbie.

The study also found that a female therapist's facial attractiveness affected a patient's comfort with self-disclosure. Obviously Justice wouldn't have been more open with his ex-wife as his physical therapist, but perhaps he might have opened up more if Kelly had been beautiful....

Don't even go there, she warned herself.

But once started, the thoughts were hard to rein in. Kelly knew firsthand how popular culture valued the attractiveness of women. She'd grown up in a household where beautiful was good. It followed that anything less than beautiful was therefore bad, or at least, less good.

Kelly had certainly felt "less good" than her sister.

Okay, so she still had some issues on this subject. But she'd come a long way from the insecure teenager to whom Mrs. Wilder had reached out a helping hand.

Kelly knew her own strengths. She also knew her weaknesses. And feeling insecure when compared to Barbie was one of those weaknesses. She usually hid it well, but sometimes it sneaked up on her, like now...and made her feel vulnerable.

Which was stupid. Logically Kelly knew it was stupid. Logically she knew she had things her sister didn't—a strong sense of purpose and accomplishment, a career she loved, a circle of close friends who genuinely cared about her.

But that didn't change the past—the way her parents had always seemed to love Barbie a bit more, the way Kelly's high school math teacher had told Kelly to be more outgoing so she'd be more popular like her sister, Barbie, the way no man she'd ever gone with who'd met her sister had ever reacted the same way toward Kelly as they had toward Barbie.

After Kelly had introduced Dave, the last man she'd been serious about, to her sister, he'd suddenly started saying things like, *Have you ever thought of changing your hair color to blonde? Have you ever thought about wearing more makeup?* And finally the real kicker, *Can't you make more effort to look nicer?*

Upon realizing that his comments were whittling away her self-confidence, Kelly had broken up with Dave a few weeks later. That had been two months ago, and it had been a difficult time for her—dredging up all her previous insecurities about her looks.

And now here she was with Justice, her sister's ex-husband. Someone else who had chosen Barbie over Kelly.

Barbie had claimed she was the one who divorced Justice, and Kelly believed her. Justice wasn't the kind of man to give up easily. Her sister was.

Or perhaps it was more accurate to say that Barbie was always moving on. She'd get bored with a job or a city or a man, and she'd move on. Looking for perfection, she would laughingly tell Kelly. "And I'll find it, too," her sister had added.

Kelly had no doubt of that. If Barbie wanted perfection, she'd get it, as she'd gotten anything she'd ever wanted. Barbie seemed to have found perfection in her Atlanta fiancé and was currently totally wrapped up in elaborate wedding plans for her August nuptials.

Kelly was glad for her sister, she truly was. But Barbie lived in "Barbie's World" and rarely took notice of what went on outside that limited sphere. Which was a good thing in this case. It meant that Kelly could come here without arousing suspicions at home. Her father thought Kelly was taking a vacation, and she aimed on keeping it that way. He wouldn't understand her being here.

At moments like this Kelly wondered if *she* understood her being here. Looking over at Justice, she remembered his comment about emotions clouding judgment. She could certainly vouch for that. As long as she did not allow her emotions, whatever they might be, to cloud her judgment where Justice was concerned, she'd be fine.

Meanwhile, all this self-introspection had made her hungry. "So what were you planning on making for dinner tonight?" she asked Justice.

"I make a mean chili."

"Sounds good."

And so they made their way into the kitchen, leaving the dog outside to gaze at them. "I'll bring you out some later," Kelly promised the animal. "Just don't tell the big, bad Marine."

"I heard that," Justice informed her.

"I meant you to," she said with a grin.

Kelly and Justice worked surprisingly well together. She anticipated things that might be difficult for him with his injury, and smoothly accomplished them before he could comment or protest.

Once they sat down, she said, "This really is a lovely place. It was nice of your friend to lend it to you."

Few people referred to "Striker" Kozlowski as

"nice." Justice met Striker in a Fort Bragg training course called Special Forces Target Acquisition and Exploitation. They'd both learned things they couldn't talk about, things that kept them alive, things that civilians wouldn't understand.

Noting Justice's preoccupied expression, she teased him. "Are you planning tomorrow's menu? Waffles for breakfast?"

"Dreamer."

"Then what were you thinking?"

He couldn't tell her the truth, that would be too close to talking about those emotions he wasn't allowed to have, so he said the first outrageous thing he could think of. "I was thinking of challenging you to a game of strip Scrabble. But then I reconsidered."

Kelly refused to let him rattle her. "Smart move. I'd win."

"In your dreams," he countered.

"I'm the one with the prodigious vocabulary."

"Oh, like I'm some big dumb Marine, huh? Fine. Put your money, or in this case your clothes, where your mouth is."

Rats, she couldn't back out now. "Fine."

"Fine."

As he retrieved the game box from the shelf beneath the bookcase, Kelly reminded herself that this wasn't about her inability to walk away from a challenge, it was about maintaining control. If she gave Justice an inch, he'd take a mile—if she showed weakness, he'd see that as his chance to wrestle control from her.

Unlike poker, she had no tricks up her sleeve where this game was concerned. She only had her own good memory and love of language to count on…and the fact that she'd played innumerable games with her hospital buddies and had won the hospital championship last month.

"Okay," Kelly said, "if you're serious about this game, then you need to understand the terminology."

"Which isn't to be trifled with, right?"

"Right. Now during the game I may balance my rack…"

Justice almost choked on his beer.

"Are you okay?" she asked.

He coughed and nodded.

"This is my rack." She pointed to the wooden shelf that held the letter tiles.

"I knew that."

"Then you also know about hot spots?"

Having just taken another swig of beer, Justice choked again. "What kind of question is that?"

"I'm referring to areas of the board that have excellent bonus-scoring opportunities."

"I knew that, too."

"Good, then since it appears that you already know everything, you can go first."

An hour later Justice was left sitting in his military shorts and nothing else.

"I guess the best woman has won yet again," Kelly noted with a triumphant grin.

Chapter Five

After last night's game of strip Scrabble, Justice didn't get much sleep. He couldn't believe Kelly had conned him again. Once more he'd been careful to make sure she hadn't cheated. She hadn't. She'd just outmaneuvered him. Right out of his pants.

It had been a disconcerting experience. A Marine never fails. No excuses, no exceptions.

Just as disconcerting had been his reaction to Kelly, who, while she'd won, hadn't gotten away completely unscathed. The memory of her stripping off her shirt to reveal the skinny pink cotton camisole beneath still made him hot. And that freaked him even worse than losing.

Justice couldn't believe the way she'd gotten to him. It's not as if he hadn't seen women with more attributes wearing far less. But there was just something about Kelly, about the way she'd sat there across the table from him with a big grin on her face, her big brown eyes shining, her wavy caramel-colored hair coming undone from its braid. Just as he'd come undone.

He couldn't let her get to him. He'd already had his heart broken once by a Hart woman, there was no way he was ever leaving himself open to that kind of pain again.

Of course, the fact that she aroused him didn't mean his heart had to be involved at all. But even her having the ability to stimulate his anatomy and his sexual fantasies gave Kelly too much power over him.

Had she deliberately tried to tempt him in the hopes of ingratiating herself even further into his life? He still wasn't completely buying the story about her being there simply because his mother had asked her to come. There was something else going on, something she wasn't telling him. He sensed that much, and he'd always been one to trust his instincts.

Granted, those instincts had been blinded by his love for Barbie, but he'd been a horny teenager in those days. Now he was a seasoned warrior in his early thirties.

A seasoned warrior with the hots for his ex-wife's younger sister.

Justice had to get some air. Being cooped up in the small beach house with Kelly was wearing him down. She was everywhere. He could smell her fresh perfume when he walked in the bathroom, hear her humming in the shower while he drank his coffee in the kitchen, see her tumbled sleeping bag on the couch and imagine himself lying beside her with her naked skin pressed against his....

He muttered as hot coffee sloshed over his good

hand. Slamming the coffee mug on the table, he pushed away from the table and headed for the front door.

"Where are you going?" Kelly inquired from the hallway.

Spotting a fishing pole near the door he said the first thing that came into his mind. "Fishing." Too late it occurred to him that his inability to lift his right arm very high might affect his ability to fish. Too bad. He wasn't about to back down now.

He waited for her to point out that fishing was a dumb idea, given his injury. He'd already prepared his comeback, that he'd use his left hand—although he shuddered to think what that would be like. Talk about ugly fishing. Given the fact that he wasn't ambidextrous, he'd probably end up with a fish hook in his own back.

But Kelly surprised him yet again. "Fishing?" she said, all bright-eyed and bouncy. She was wearing denim cutoffs that showed off her long, tanned legs and a red tank top. Her hair was loose for once, which only increased her image as a sexy temptress in his view. "I'll come with you."

"No way," Justice stated emphatically.

She blinked at him. "Why not?"

He clearly couldn't tell her the truth, that he needed to get away from the temptation she presented. So instead he said, "You'll scare all the fish away with your constant talking."

"I will not. And I don't talk constantly."

"There's no way you could be quiet long enough."

"Want to bet?"

Red flags immediately went up in his head. "Betting with you has already gotten me into trouble."

"You're just upset because you lost."

"I'm used to winning."

"Then consider this a learning experience."

"I don't intend to learn how to lose." He shifted the fishing rod to his left hand, aggravated by the continuing lack of strength in his injured arm.

"How about this? If I talk while you're fishing then I make dinner tonight."

"It's your turn to make dinner tonight, anyway," he replied.

"Okay, then I agree to make dinner tomorrow night, as well. I'll make vegetable lasagna. My specialty."

"How can you make something like that with what I have in the house?"

"Because I brought the ingredients with me, a bottle of my homemade sauce, some cheese, some pasta. Lasagna is my comfort food. As good as chicken soup for whatever ails you."

"Sounds like you plan ahead."

"I try to. So what do you say?"

"Make that a pledge to make dinner for the rest of the week and you're on."

"Deal." She nodded, her hair sliding off her bare shoulders and her question-mark jewelry clinking.

"Your earrings are too noisy," Justice noted.

She rolled her eyes. "I don't believe you. Fine, I'll take off my earrings. But I'm not taking off anything else," she warned him. "This isn't strip Scrabble."

She gathered her hair up and tucked it under a denim baseball cap she'd just dug out of her backpack. Justice was still recovering his breath from eyeing her tempting backside and watching the way her cutoffs rode up the back of her thighs when she'd bent over her backpack.

"You ready?" she asked in that perky voice of hers.

He nodded, keeping his face impassive, and headed out the door with his fishing pole and gear in hand.

Kelly followed him, very well aware that something was eating at him. She couldn't believe his brooding mood was caused by him being a poor loser. She'd tried watching Justice's face in an attempt to decipher his thoughts. She should have known it would be an impossible task. He had his warrior mask in place.

But there was no denying the fire in his vivid blue eyes or the impatience emanating from his lean body. She might not know what was upsetting him, but something clearly was.

He was wearing shorts and another one of Striker's Hawaiian shirts. This morning the shorts were navy blue and the shirt orange and yellow. As she watched him walk down the sandy path, she told herself that her interest in him was purely professional. She wanted to confirm that he wasn't limping from their workout yesterday. But her appreciation of his male form was purely feminine.

She'd never been one to swoon over a guy's anatomy, and while she certainly wasn't swooning now over his, she was grinning in admiration at the way his shorts fit his buns of steel.

Turning to look over his shoulder, he eyed her suspiciously. "What are you staring at?"

She wondered what he'd say if she replied that she was staring at him and his buns. Unfortunately, she wasn't bold enough to find out. Instead she said, "Your legs are healing nicely."

He nodded curtly and moved on, away from the ocean.

"We're surrounded by water, why are you heading inland to go fishing?" Kelly asked.

She saw his shoulders heave in a sigh. "I knew you couldn't be quiet."

"The bet only begins once we arrive at the fishing site."

"Striker told me about a good place, a stream inland."

"Is he a Marine, too?"

Justice nodded.

"Is everyone you know a Marine?"

"Negative. I know a few squids, too."

Kelly frowned. "Squids?"

"Navy personnel."

"What about civilians? Do you know many of them?"

He turned and confronted her. "Why this interrogation about my private life?"

She shrugged. "I was just making conversation."

"Well, don't." He started walking again. "The fish don't like it."

She skipped to keep up with his long strides. "I've never gone fishing before. My dad used to promise me he'd take me with him when I was a kid, but my mother didn't feel it was a proper pastime for a girl. How many people live on this island?" she asked as they eventually passed another house, the first she'd seen since leaving his beach house.

"Not many. That's why I came here."

He paused at a stand in front of the house, picked up a small box and stuffed some money in a glass jar there. "What's that?"

"Bait."

"They just sell bait out of their beach house?"

"You're just full of questions, aren't you. Striker told me he gets bait here."

"There's no store or town or anything?"

"There's a marina on the other side that has a couple of gas tanks and a small store for essential items."

"Really? Maybe we should check that out sometime."

"Why?" Justice asked.

"For some interaction."

He turned to look at her, one of his dark eyebrows lifting over his intense blue eyes. "Getting tired of my company already?"

"No, that's not it."

"You didn't run out of some kind of feminine thing, did you?"

"No." Kelly refused to blush. "I just thought it might be nice to look around while I was here."

"Why? It's not like you're on vacation."

"Actually I told my dad I was on vacation," she admitted, "resting up at a friend's beach house."

"Why would you do that?"

"I didn't think he'd understand the truth."

Justice wasn't sure he understood it, either. Sure, she'd claimed she'd come to repay a debt to his mom, because of a secret friendship they'd been carrying on over the years unbeknownst to him and apparently to anyone else. But was that really it? Or did Kelly have some kind of hidden agenda coming here?

It was hard for him not to be suspicious of her motives. He was naturally suspicious of everyone. It went with the territory in his line of work. In Special Ops—Special Operations—your fellow Marines were your only friends, and everyone else had to be considered a foe. Infiltrating hostile territory to undertake covert activities meant that you always had to be on guard.

The one time he'd relaxed his guard had been that fateful day outside Camp Lejeune when he'd been driving to meet friends and had seen the accident.

He switched off those thoughts. There was no point in rehashing the past. He had to deal with the present.

His Force Recon buddy Striker had understood Justice's need to get away and had offered him the use of the beach house, no questions asked. Unlike Kelly, who was full of questions. She was asking them again now, this time about Striker.

"Tell me more about your Marine buddy who owns the beach house."

"Why?"

"Because I'd like to learn more about him. Is he married?"

That question threw him. "No."

"I didn't think so."

"What's that supposed to mean?"

"It means that the beach house didn't appear to have a woman's touch, which made me think your friend was single. What's he look like?"

"Why? Did you want me to fix you up with him?"

"I already told you that overbearing Marines aren't my type."

"Maybe Striker is the one who could change your mind."

"Maybe he is," she infuriated him by saying. "So what's he look like?"

"Dark hair, green eyes. The women all like him."

"Ah, a womanizer like your brothers, huh?"

"Two of my brothers are hitched," Justice reminded her. "Joe and Prudence are expecting their first baby later this year."

"So your mom told me."

"Right. You and my mom being so close." His voice was clearly mocking.

"You're not still suspicious about that, are you?"

"I'm suspicious about everything," Justice replied.

"But you trust this Striker friend of yours?"

"With my life."

"Why? Because he's a Marine like you?"

"Because he's proved his loyalty and because he doesn't bombard me with questions." Justice stepped up his pace.

The trail wound through swaying sawgrass and under ancient live oaks and tropical palmetto. It felt good to be out of the house and on the move.

"Did you know that Spanish moss is actually part of the pineapple family?" Kelly said, pointing to the long festoons hanging from a nearby gnarled tree branch. "It actually draws all its nourishment from the air so it's not a parasite and doesn't kill trees."

She was doing it again. Talking. Showing him

how smart she was, how uninformed he was. *Do I look like the kind of guy who cares about Spanish moss?* he wanted to growl at her, but didn't. Because she was so endearing when she listed her bits of trivia.

Endearing? Justice was sure this was a first. He'd never referred to a woman as endearing before. It was Kelly's fault. Her use of words like trifling and trouncing made him think of endearing. Or maybe it was her light-up-the-sky smile and root-beer-popsicle-brown eyes. He'd always been a sucker for root-beer popsicles.

Not that he intended on being a sucker for Kelly. No way, no how.

Justice found the creek without any trouble ten minutes later. Discouraging Kelly from chatting cheerfully was not as easy. She looked as eager as a kid when he handed her the fishing reel to hold while he prepared the bait.

That eagerness turned to dismay when she saw what he held in his hand.

"That's a worm." She lifted her big soulful eyes to his. "You're not going to put that sharp hook through that little worm, are you? That's cruel. Can't you use something else, like one of those feather thingies? I'll bet the fish would like to bite on that more than this poor worm."

"You mean this poor worm?" He wiggled the worm in front of her nose. She didn't flinch. Instead she touched his left hand and removed the worm from his clasp.

His surprise wasn't caused by her actions as much as it was by his own response to her touch. She'd touched him yesterday and he'd been fine.

But that was before his stupid idea of strip Scrabble last night. Seeing her in that skimpy camisole had left an indelible mark on him, making him see her as a female and not simply as Barbie's baby sister.

In fact, there was nothing babyish about her. She was all woman. Shapely in all the right places. Much more curvaceous than her sister, who'd always prided herself on her thin body.

"It's all right, baby."

It took Justice a second to realize that Kelly was cooing to the stupid worm, not to him.

"I won't let him hurt you. There you go." She carefully lowered the worm from her cupped hand to the ground, away from the path along the side of the creek. "You're free now. Live long and prosper."

"You're using Spock's saying from *Star Trek* on a worm?"

"Yes. Spock would never have picked on a poor defenseless worm."

"We're going fishing here," he reminded her. "That means catching fish."

"Yes, but you let them go as soon as you catch them, right?"

"Wrong. What would be the point in that?"

"I don't know, but I read some article once in a magazine about fishing and it said they let them go."

"Trout fishing out west maybe. That's not what we're doing here." It was actually doubtful he'd catch anything, given the fact that he had to use his left arm. He'd be lucky if he even got the line into the water. Obviously this hadn't been one of his brighter ideas.

"We've got enough food in the house for now, it's not like you have to catch a fish or starve. You're not on some deserted tropical island or anything."

"Don't I wish," Justice muttered. "We had a bet, remember?"

"Right." She gently dumped out the remaining worms from the box. "That I wouldn't talk while you were fishing. But you're not fishing yet. You're still preparing to fish."

"No thanks to you, letting my bait loose."

"The rest of the worms had to join Fred."

"Fred?"

"Fred the worm. They had to join him or they'd get lost and never find each other. You can't separate a family like that."

Justice rolled his eyes. "They're worms."

"That doesn't mean they can't have family ties."

"You are definitely going to lose this bet. I can taste that lasagna dinner tonight."

"Fine, then you don't need to eat a fish tonight. My lasagna tastes better, anyway. Who knows where that fish you might have caught has been?"

He stared at her in amazement. "I don't believe you."

"Have you started fishing yet?"

"Yes."

She watched as he awkwardly checked the feathered lure already on the fishing rod. The truth was he'd never been much of a fisherman and had only gone once or twice as a kid. He knew one end of the fishing pole from the other, but that was about the extent of his knowledge. Not that he was about to admit that to her.

"Okay, then I'll start talking now," she announced.

"*Start* talking? You haven't stopped since we left the beach house."

"Did you know that they've done studies on how many words a man uses in a day and how many a woman uses, and women use a lot more?"

"That's a no-brainer. Any guy could have told the researchers that."

"The sexes just have completely different ways of communicating," she said.

The reality of her talking about sex made his body tighten. Erotic images flashed through his mind with rapid-fire intensity—Kelly naked, her wavy caramel hair tumbling down past her shoulders, the tips of her breasts peeking out from beneath the silky strands.

"Here, hold this a second." He shoved the fishing rod at her.

"Isn't the line supposed to be in the water?"

"Yes."

"Can I do that?" she asked all eager-eyed again.

"Sure. Go for it." He made sure to step out of range as she enthusiastically cast her line into the water. Then he tried to look busy—not easy to do, given the fact that the only prop he had was the empty box he'd gotten the worms in. Striker had a fishing gear box but Justice had left it back at the beach house.

It wasn't as if he'd planned this fishing expedition. It had been a completely spur-of-the-moment thing. He couldn't even lift a fishing pole with his right arm. How pitiful was that? He who carried grenade launchers over treacherous terrain.

He tested his injured arm, trying to work through the pain. Sweat broke out on his forehead.

"I've got something!" Kelly shrieked. "What do I do? Reel it in?" Next thing he knew, she'd reeled in a respectable-size fish. "Quick, let him loose. He can't breathe out here in the air. Don't hurt him." She aimed the scaly thing at Justice, almost smacking him in the face with it. "Hurry, hurry. No, wait. That's not good for your arm. I'll do it. Tell me what to do."

"Just give me the fish," Justice growled.

She held back. "Only if you promise not to hurt him."

"Give me the fish." He spaced the words out in a voice that made his newest recruits tremble.

She wasn't the least bit intimidated. "Do you promise not to hurt him?"

"I promise. Now give me the damn fish."

"I thought Marines weren't supposed to swear."

"They can do so in certain extenuating circumstances, and you are definitely an extenuating circumstance. There." Justice released the fish, hiding a grimace as the movement aggravated his arm.

She quickly took the fish from him and slid it back into the water. Turning to face him again, she grinned. "There now, wasn't that fun?"

"Are you asking me or the fish?"

"You."

"Oh, yeah, that was a real barrel of laughs." He said the words with wry humor.

"Thank you for letting him go." Kelly reached up to kiss his cheek just as Justice turned his head to reply. The end result was that her lips brushed his mouth.

Instant electricity. Unimaginable power. Sizzling heat.

The contact annihilated all Kelly's preconceived ideas of what a kiss could or should be like. She'd planned on a fleeting caress that was there, then gone. Instead she'd gotten more than she'd bargained for as his mouth consumed hers with unexpected passion.

He tasted of coffee and sexy male. His lips moved against hers in a sensual interplay. She closed her eyes, losing herself in the moment—in his hunger, in her desire. The hot sun poured down on them, but it couldn't compare to the fiery warmth uncoiling deep within her body.

Kelly couldn't believe this moment had come, that it wasn't a dream. It was almost too good to be real. But nothing she could have dreamed would have prepared her for the most passionate kiss imaginable. She could feel her own heart beating out of control and was shaken to realize that his was beating equally strongly beneath her hands, which she'd placed on his chest in startled surprise at first but left them there with awed appreciation.

His hand rested on her shoulder, heating her bare skin, each caressing fingertip stirring up a firestorm of temptation. He was holding her without embracing her, captivating her completely with the sheer force of his kiss.

He drew her closer, shifting his hand to her neck where he cupped the curve of her jaw. He brushed his thumb against the outer corner of her mouth. She shivered with delight as he coaxed her lips to part.

The kiss shifted to a new level of intimacy now, one that was dangerously seductive.

What was she doing? The thought rose up and smacked her out of the romantic moment. What was she doing kissing Justice, letting him kiss her? This was exactly what she was supposed to avoid.

She'd started this, she had to end it, before she melted into his arms and things got completely out of control. In the end they both pulled back at the same moment.

Kelly pressed trembling fingers to her lips, as if to keep the memory of his kiss there forever.

"I'm sorry," she whispered, not even sure quite what it was she was apologizing for.

"Forget it," Justice said, his voice as curt and unemotional as ever. "It won't happen again."

But Kelly knew she'd never forget their kiss, not if she lived to be 150.

Chapter Six

Unlike the walk out, the walk back to the beach house was accomplished in almost total silence.

That didn't diminish the tension, it only seemed to enhance it. At least, that's how Kelly felt. She had no idea what Justice was thinking. He had his Marine face on.

Having told her that it wouldn't happen again, Justice clearly had no interest in repeating the kiss they'd shared. Neither did she. Analyzing it, however, was another thing. The only way to learn not to repeat past mistakes was to learn from them. So what had she learned from that awesome kiss?

For one thing she'd discovered that Justice was the most incredible kisser on the face of the entire planet. The mere memory of his mouth consuming hers made her weak at the knees once again. Not a helpful bit of information. Unless it served to remind her that she was vulnerable where Justice was concerned. For whatever reason. Hormones, a full moon, leftovers of an adolescent crush—whatever the reason, she had a weak spot for him. A very hot weak spot.

She felt her cheeks flush. Time to yank out her "sensible" protective shield. Justice was a normal healthy male, who was clearly an accomplished kisser. He obviously wanted her to act as if nothing had happened between them. Which was a logical thing to do. Much better than getting in over their heads.

Not that Justice was suffering from the same vulnerability that was making her heart race. He showed no signs of brooding about the incident. He'd probably already completely erased it from his memory banks. Men were like that. They had the uncanny ability to wipe out anything even vaguely approaching emotional territory.

Her own father had often done that. The closest he'd come to showing emotion had been to give her an awkward pat on the shoulder. Which she had to assume was meant to be taken as a sign of paternal affection. But it sure didn't take the place of being told once in a while that you were loved.

Not that love or even affection had anything to do with Justice kissing her. She just happened to be…handy. That had to have been it. Besides, she'd been the one who'd reached for him. Granted, she'd merely planned on planting a platonic kiss on his cheek, but still, she'd been the one who'd started it all.

But he was the one who'd set the pace for their kiss once their lips had met. He hadn't turned away from her.

Which meant what? That when a woman throws

herself at him, he responds. Big deal. Few men wouldn't respond.

But he'd certainly responded...passionately. And being the woman she was, that made her wonder if he hadn't been thinking of Barbie when he kissed her.

Kelly shot him a covert look from beneath her lashes before remembering she was wearing sunglasses and could stare at him outright without him knowing it. He'd already vehemently denied that he was still pining after her sister. And, as a practical matter, the divorce had happened twelve years ago—which was a long time for anyone to pine. But if someone had emotions that ran deep, as she suspected Justice's did, then time didn't matter.

Rats. Couldn't the man do something to give her a clue as to his thoughts? Couldn't he have said something?

Or even better, couldn't he have been a sloppy kisser? Couldn't he have left her cold, not tempted her in the tiniest bit? None of this was working out as she'd planned.

The plan had been to get in, help Justice with his physical therapy and get out. There hadn't been anything in her plan about being kissed senseless by him.

Okay, one thing was clear here. She kept harping on it, she knew, but facts were facts. Justice hadn't reached for her first, she'd reached for him. She was no sexy vixen who'd tempted him so badly that he could no longer resist, had tossed his fishing pole aside and had grabbed her in his arms and kissed her. The very idea of such a thing made her smile.

Which was a good thing. That meant she hadn't lost her sense of humor along with her sanity.

"What are you smiling at?" Justice asked suspiciously.

Maybe he was as curious about her thoughts as she was about his? Doubtful, but within the distant realm of possibility. The *very* distant realm. The reality was that Justice was still distrustful of her, suspicious of what she might be up to.

Good. Maybe that would make him a little unsettled. It wasn't fair that she was the only one feeling as if she had a cement mixer for a stomach.

Unfortunately, Kelly was too softhearted to wish her own uncertainties on Justice. So she answered his question. Sort of. "I guess I was smiling at human foibles."

"Foibles? Another of your trifling words?" His voice was mocking.

"Just remember who beat the pants off you at word games, fella."

She'd meant her comment to be a strictly teasing one, but the memory of him wearing nothing but his boxer shorts was making her all hot and bothered again.

"That's not something I'm likely to forget," Justice said.

"Me, neither," she said truthfully.

"So when are you going to give me the chance to win?"

"Never. We've done all the stripping we're going to do."

A sensible comment if ever she'd spoken one, but somehow what stuck in Kelly's mind was *we* and *stripping*—the image of her and Justice peeling off their clothing as they continued the kiss that had sparked off her hormones earlier.

"Stripping is definitely off-limits," Justice agreed.

Kelly had to nod, her mouth was too dry at the erotic images wickedly flashing in her wayward mind.

"Much too tempting," he added.

What was that supposed to mean? She wanted to pounce on his words. Had he been tempted by the possibility of her stripping? Jeez, how desperate did that make her sound? Like he wouldn't be tempted by any woman stripping in front of him.

Get a grip, she sternly ordered herself. And not a grip on this sexy Marine. A grip on your self-control.

"Someday we'll look back on last night and laugh," she said with manufactured cheerfulness.

"I don't think so."

She didn't think so, either. This time she couldn't resist asking, "Why not?"

"Because I don't like losing."

Oh, right. How could she have forgotten that element of it? Here she was all wrapped up in the stripping part, and all he could think of was winning. A Marine never fails. Even at board games.

"I don't like losing, either." And I must be losing my mind to have thought for one minute that Justice had found me deliciously tempting. The thought burned through her psyche. Her...the sensible, smart Hart sister? Deliciously tempting? Not likely. Maybe he *had* been thinking about Barbie when he'd kissed her. That thought made Kelly want to crawl into a hole.

"Something we agree on, then."

"What is?" She'd lost track of their conversation, consumed as she was with the wave of humiliation that she was determined to hide from him at all costs.

"That neither of us likes losing."

"Right." She nodded curtly. "You know what, why don't you go on ahead?" Her words were choppy but she didn't care. "I think I'm going to head over to the beach for a while and collect some shells." She veered off without waiting for his reply.

There was a time to stand firm and a time to cut your losses and retreat in order to fight another day.

The only problem was that Kelly's fight was with herself and her attraction to Justice...and it didn't look like a battle that she was winning at the moment.

For the next day or two Kelly made a point of keeping her relationship with Justice strictly professional. She touched him as little as possible, showing him the exercises she wanted him to complete rather than using her usual hands-on approach. But she did have to touch him on occasion, and when she did so, she deliberately acted as if he were a nonsexual buddy she'd known for years, someone she was as comfortable with as an old pair of slippers.

It didn't really work. At least not in her own mind. The memory of that fiery kiss they'd shared remained as vivid as ever. But hopefully Justice had no idea that she tossed and turned at night over him.

She did catch him looking at her sometimes, however. She referred to this as his "secret" stare, but then, he was a man with a history of secrets and covert operations. There was no way of knowing what he was thinking about when he looked at her, or if he was even seeing her at all. For all she knew, he could have been thinking about something else entirely.

She did know Justice was frustrated by the slowness of his recovery. She also knew he was still pushing himself, despite her warning him that doing so was not helpful.

They'd talked about setting goals that first day they'd started his therapy. "My goal is to return to Force Recon," he'd said.

"I thought perhaps we could start with some smaller goals," she'd replied. "Other patients have started with tasks they'd like to perform."

"Okay, I'd like to be able to do a hundred one-armed push-ups."

"That wasn't quite what I had in mind. My other patients have started with specific things like tossing money into the toll booth, or retrieving their ATM card from the machine, both of which include lifting their arms…"

The dark look on his face had made her voice trail off. In the end he had come up with some smaller goals that involved range of motion, but it had been a struggle.

The thing was, they were stuck together in a relatively small space—the beach house. There were no further visits from what Justice called the turtle women. Kelly had taken to walking the beach by herself every day, usually right before sunset. The mystery dog accompanied her each time, running after driftwood she'd toss for him and bringing it back to her with a joyful bark. She'd been slipping him food every day, but Justice clearly didn't approve.

He told her so again now, as she returned from her walk with the animal loping merrily by her side. Seeing Justice's disapproving look, Kelly said, "The dog is just keeping me company."

"I told you that the aforementioned canine does not belong to me and is not to be babied. You're not doing him any favors by making him dependent on handouts. He needs to fend for himself, to make his own way."

"We're not talking about one of your Marine recruits here, we're talking about a dog. He's not even that big yet, are you, fella?" Kelly rubbed the animal's ears, which earned her an adoring look.

"Little, big, it doesn't matter. You're making him soft. You're not going to be here very long. I've seen it happen before with military personnel and their dependents, leaving animals behind when they're shipped out."

"I wouldn't abandon an animal or anyone I love." Not the way my sister abandoned you, Kelly wanted to add but didn't. "I'd stick like glue to someone I love."

"Easy to say, not so easy to do," Justice noted cynically.

"I never said it would be easy," she pointed out. "If I was into 'easy' I wouldn't have become a physical therapist. There's nothing easy about this job."

"Then why do you do it?"

"Because I can make a difference in people's lives. Isn't that why you do what you do?"

He shrugged.

"You don't think what you do makes a difference in people's lives?"

He was a warrior. She was a healer. They were coming from two entirely opposite places. His mission was to search and destroy, hers was to touch and restore.

"I don't think about it," Justice said curtly. Which was true. He kept his thoughts and emotions in a black box and didn't delve inside of it. It was a box that carried one of those warnings like the microwave in the kitchen—"Do not remove back cover on danger of electric shock." His internal black box was the permanent dumping ground for all his toxic thoughts.

Justice had no idea what it was about a man's emotions that made women so itchy to tamper with them. Maybe they just liked playing with a guy's mind. They usually started out with the dreaded *We have to talk...*

You *had* to breathe, but you never *had* to talk. At least none of the guys he knew did. Maybe some touchy-feely guys liked exploring their emotions, but then, most touchy-feely guys didn't become United States Marines.

As far as Justice was concerned, emotional self-examination was both risky and unnecessary. Risky because he might reveal something that would make him vulnerable.

As if able to read his thoughts, Kelly said, "There's something I've been meaning to talk to you about."

Her words were close enough to *We have to talk* to make him uncomfortable. Justice was tempted to begin immediate evasive action—something along the lines of starting an argument, although staring blankly into space also worked pretty well in his experience with women. Not with Kelly, though. Nothing seemed to stop her when she got that gleam in her root-beer-colored eyes.

He braced himself for her next barrage of questions.

"We need more food," she said.

"Food?" he repeated blankly.

"Yes. Food. Sustenance. You know, the stuff we eat for breakfast, lunch and dinner. We're running out. I thought maybe we could walk over to that store you told me about tomorrow."

Justice practically heaved an internal sigh of relief. Food. This was a problem he could easily solve. "I'll give you the money and you can go order whatever you think we'll need. They deliver."

"I can't go by myself. I'm directionally challenged. I'd get lost for sure."

"We're on an island. How lost can you get?"

"You'd be surprised. You have to come with me. Is there some reason you don't want to?" she challenged him.

"I'm not into shopping."

"We're not going shopping. Think of it as restocking provisions. That sounds like a military operation, doesn't it?"

"Not one Force Recon would be involved with."

"Well then, this will be yet another learning experience for you," Kelly declared with that cheerful yet sexy grin of hers. "Unless there's something else you're not telling me? Some reason going there would make you uneasy?"

Uneasy? Marines didn't get uneasy. Justice knew he'd been outmaneuvered. He also suspected that this might turn out to be yet another so-called learning experience that would end up with Kelly getting the upper hand unless he took action to prevent that.

An ounce of prevention was worth a pound of cure. And Justice was determined to prevent Kelly from gaining any more inroads into his psyche. He would put up whatever road blocks necessary.

Kelly walked outside the beach house the next morning to a gorgeous day. The blue sky held a puffy cloud or two to add interest without getting in the way of the sunshine. A salty breeze teased the clumps of sea oats growing along the dunes and set them swaying in a horticultural ballet. Seagulls scavenged for food along the water's edge, their feet creating a delicate embroidery on the wet sand.

It was one of those days that made you feel glad to be alive.

Justice didn't look glad about anything. He stood in front of her, wearing jeans and one of Striker's Hawaiian shirts in blues and whites, looking dangerously sexy. The laid-back shirts might suit his buddy's temperament, but they were definitely at odds with Justice's darker side. He just wasn't a beach-bum, surfer-guy type.

Kelly wondered what Justice saw when he looked at the scenery. Did he view the sea oats as a place for an enemy to hide? Did he ever see the beauty in his surroundings or only the possibilities for danger?

"It must be a tough way to live."

Kelly didn't realize she'd murmured the words aloud until Justice said, "Being a Marine?"

"Always being on alert, training yourself to think of everything around you as a weapon. That doesn't leave much room for the beautiful things in life."

"I leave that stuff to other people."

"Yes, I know, but look at what you're missing." She waved her hand at the view in front of them. "Tell me what you see."

"A beach, the ocean, camouflage locations in the foliage—"

"I knew it," she interrupted him. "Those are sea oats, and look how they're dancing in the warm breeze."

He looked at her as if she were crazy before drawling, "Dancing sea oats aren't my thing."

"No, turning forks into weapons is your thing."

"Is there a reason we're having this conversation?"

"It just bothers me, that's all."

"My being a Marine bothered your sister, too."

"It's not about being a Marine, Justice. It's about feeding your soul so it doesn't shrivel up and die. It's about letting some light into the dark places."

Justice mentally shoved her words aside. What did Kelly know about dark places? She didn't have a clue. And she certainly didn't have a clue about *his* dark places. No one did. And Justice aimed on keeping it that way.

"Welcome, folks," a burly man in a white T-shirt and denim overalls greeted them as soon as they walked in the building named Earl's. "How can I help you?"

"We came to get a few supplies," Kelly replied. "We're getting low on food."

Earl smiled. "Well now, we can't have that, can we? You just head right on back there and fill up on some good eats. You folks staying here on the island?"

"That's right." She would have said more, but a warning look from Justice prevented her.

"We don't get many tourists here. My name's Earl Bodine, how about you?"

"I'm Kelly and this is Justice."

The older man gave Justice a frown. "Have we met before?"

"No," Justice said curtly.

"Your face sure seems familiar to me." Earl frowned. "I never forget a face. Seems like I've seen you on TV. Not on *America's Most Wanted*...it was local news. Justice...unusual name." His expression changed as recognition came. "Hey, boy, you're that Marine that saved that baby, aren't you? You are. I knew I'd seen you before. Well now, we don't get many bona fide heroes in here. Hey, Al!" he yelled at a man in the back of the store. "This here's Justice, a bona fide hero!"

"I'm not a hero," Justice denied in a gritty voice.

"Sure you are, the TV said so. I'll bet the Marines will give you some kind of medal or something. I was in the army myself back in the Korean War." He was interrupted by the arrival of two more customers. "Listen up, this here's Justice, the Marine that saved that little boy's life. It was all on TV. He's a bona fide hero."

Justice couldn't believe it. The place had been practically deserted two minutes ago and now people were coming out of the woodwork—from the boat dock, from the backroom. All of them slapping him on the back, hailing him as a hero.

He hated it. Hated living a lie. Sure he'd saved a kid's life, but he was no hero.

Because the question that he kept hidden in that dark place inside him was, Would he do the same thing again, knowing he might risk his future with Force Recon? And the answer that was eating him up inside was that he didn't know. He didn't know if he'd do the same thing again.

Ask him if he'd risk death by deploying out on a dangerous mission with Force Recon tomorrow and the answer was an immediate and heartfelt yes. He'd risk death. For the greater good. The needs of the many outweighed the needs of the few.

That began in boot camp, where the words *I, me* or *mine* were deleted from a new recruit's vocabulary. Yet wasn't he betraying that philosophy by worrying about his own future with the Marine Corps?

Justice had always been a man who saw things in black and white, never shades of gray. Now it felt as if he were quagmired in grays, bogged down and unable to maneuver.

He wanted to shout at them all that he was no hero, that men like Earl who'd fought for their country in the Korean War, men like the rescue workers at the World Trade Center—they were the real heroes. But he couldn't say a word. He could only stand there like a wooden figure, while the words flowed around him.

Kelly noticed his rigid stance and the muscle ticking along his jaw. He was the epitome of controlled emotion. Clearly something was going on inside his head, and just as clearly he was doing everything in his power to hide it. This was more than discomfort at being called a hero. He'd practically recoiled from the use of the word.

Not that his state of mind was apparent to anyone but her. But then she was looking at him through the eyes of a woman...*A woman, what?* she asked herself. *You better not have been about to say a woman in love. Because that is not on the agenda here. You are not allowed to go down that path, no matter how tempting he might be.*

For once Kelly ignored that sensible voice inside and instead kept her focus on Justice. Quickly gathering up the groceries, she dumped them on the front counter and said, "Well, we've got to get going now. Could you add this up for us, Earl?"

"It's on the house," Earl proclaimed. "No way I'd charge a hero."

"And there's no way Justice can accept your gracious offer," Kelly said. Leaning closer to Earl, she smiled and said, "You know how these Marines are. Not wanting to be in anyone's debt, very proud and all that."

Earl nodded knowingly and whispered conspiratorially. "You're right." A little louder he said, "Okay, it's not on the house, but I'm tossing in a box of chocolates for you two newlyweds. No arguing now."

Kelly would have corrected Earl about his misconception that she and Justice were a couple, but that would have meant staying longer and she got the definite impression that Justice wanted out of there ASAP. So she held her tongue, accepted the chocolates, paid the money and smiled at Earl as Justice took both bags in his good left hand.

"Sorry about that," Kelly said once they were out of earshot of the store.

"I told you I didn't want to go there," Justice growled. "And I'll pay you back for the food as soon as we get to the beach house."

Knowing he was upset, she didn't challenge his rude tone of voice and instead kept pace with his fast march forward. She waited about five minutes before saying, "Do you want to talk about it?"

"Talk about what?"

"About why being called a hero upsets you so much."

"Drop it."

This time his curt order did irritate her. "What was I thinking? Of course a big bad Marine wouldn't want to talk about his emotions. He's not supposed to have any, right?"

By this time they'd reached a turn in the path shaded by a stand of palmettos.

"Emotions? You want emotions?" Justice dropped the plastic grocery bags onto the soft sand. "I'll show you emotions." Snagging her with his good arm, he kissed her.

Unlike the last time, he initiated this embrace. Just like last time the touch of his mouth on hers created instant heat and undeniable temptation.

But there was a new element as his tongue traced the outline of her lips before hungrily parting them to dip inside, exploring the inner softness with expert thoroughness. There was rawness here, a well of powerful emotions that caught her up and propelled her into the turbulent passion of the moment.

Held tightly against his body, her breasts were pressed against his chest. The thin cotton of his shirt and her T-shirt couldn't hide the warmth of his body, or the immediacy of her response. Her nipples tingled as she felt the hardening of his lower body beneath the placket of his jeans.

He was devouring her, eating her up with deliciously wicked thrusts of his tongue, heating her up with deliciously wicked thrusts of his hips. She ached deep inside, wanting him so badly it hurt.

Then Justice broke their embrace off as suddenly as he'd initiated it.

She blinked at him, her gaze still clouded with passion. "What was that all about?"

"Forget it."

"I don't know what to say to that."

"That would be a first," he muttered.

The passion was clearing now, and Kelly wasn't about to allow history to repeat itself. "This is the second time you've kissed me and expected me to act as if nothing happened."

"*You* kissed *me* when we were fishing."

"Oh, please." She rolled her eyes. "I'm not going to stand here and argue like kids about who kissed who first."

"Good. Because I don't want to argue with you."

"You just want to kiss me and then have me forget about it."

"Affirmative."

"Well, dream on, Marine. I *like* talking about things."

"Yeah, I noticed that. And I don't like talking about things."

"Yeah, I noticed that," she shot right back. "Tough noogies."

He lifted a dark eyebrow. "Tough noogies?"

"A physical therapist never swears," Kelly stated primly. "It shows a lack of discipline."

He had to smile at his own words being tossed back at him. "You're really something, you know that?"

He said it with some admiration, which made her have to ask, "What kind of something?"

"There you go again. Asking questions."

"And there you go, clamming up."

"Speaking of clams, maybe we should go clamming this afternoon."

She waved his words away. "Don't try to distract me with seafood. Were you complimenting me or insulting me by saying I'm really something?"

"Complimenting."

"Like you'd admit if you were insulting me," Kelly muttered.

He shrugged. "Hey, it was your question."

"Right. Let me rephrase it then. Or ask an entirely different question. Why did you kiss me?"

"You get right to the point, don't you?"

"Yes." She met his stare head-on. No way was she letting him off the hook here. "Want me to repeat the question?"

"No. And I don't want to answer it, either."

"Tough—"

"Noogies," he completed for her. "Right. Okay, you want to know why I kissed you? Because you're an incredibly sexy woman and I wanted to. Are you happy now?"

Chapter Seven

Was she happy now? Stunned was closer to the truth. Justice wanted to kiss her? Kelly didn't know what to say. "Oh."

"That's it? Just 'oh'?"

The man was mocking her. She should do something about that. The only problem was she couldn't think clearly at the moment because her brain had turned to mush. And not by his kiss but by his words. *You're an incredibly sexy woman and I wanted to kiss you.*

He had to be kidding. Men didn't call her incredibly sexy. Cute was the term they usually used.

Unless Justice had said that to throw her off track? That sounded like something he'd do. Much more likely than him actually believing she was incredibly sexy. "Oh, I get it. Clever, Justice, real clever, trying to throw me off track by saying I'm sexy."

"Why would that throw you offtrack?"

"Why would you think I'm sexy?" she countered. "Come on, I'm not a foolish teenager ready to be bowled over by fancy words."

"I didn't think they were all that fancy," he denied. "In fact, I thought they were pretty straightforward."

"So you expect me to believe that you kissed me because you found me so sexy that you had to drop the groceries and kiss me on the spot? Why now? Wasn't I this sexy thirty minutes ago when we left the beach house?"

"Actually you were sexier then," Justice replied, "because your lips were all wet and shiny in the sunlight."

His words stopped Kelly in her tracks before she narrowed her eyes suspiciously. "You're making that up. You kissed me because you were aggravated with me. Why can't you admit it?"

"I'm always aggravated with you."

"Gee, thanks. I'm always aggravated with you, too."

"Creates some powerful sparks between us, doesn't it?"

"Aggravation?"

"No, attraction." Justice picked up the discarded groceries and strolled away, leaving Kelly standing speechless beneath the swaying palmettos.

Justice had dropped a bombshell and then just walked off. For the next twenty-four hours he didn't mention their kiss again or the attraction he'd referred to. But it was like that story about the elephant in the middle of the living room—there, even if no one referred to it.

She felt the increasing sexual awareness in the way she responded to touching him, in the way he responded to her touch during their physical therapy sessions. Touch was a powerful thing. And touching Justice was a downright mighty thing—mighty dangerous.

He was such a dynamic man. And a complicated one. She still wasn't totally buying his claim that he'd kissed her because he was attracted to her. It was a tempting thought, though.

But even more than that, she wanted to know what was eating away at him, what angst was simmering inside. Because as much as he tried to hide it, she knew something was going on inside this tough Marine of hers.

Wait a second, she sternly ordered her thoughts. Justice is not *your* Marine. Let's not get too possessive here.

Too late, another internal voice warned. *You're already hooked like that fish in the creek the other day.*

That possibility made her cranky. The fact that Justice was in a similarly cranky mood was bound to create trouble sooner or later during their therapy session. Things came to a head later that afternoon.

"I'm sick of these stupid, wimpy exercises. I'm not making any progress. I can't even hold a stupid lightweight fishing pole properly, how the Sam Hill am I supposed to hold an M-16?"

"I'm assuming that's not a fishing pole?"

"It's a rifle." He said the words as if speaking to an ignorant idiot.

"I told you that there was no instant miracle cure for your injury. The shoulder is a very complex piece of machinery, made up of three bones, the scupula which is the shoulder blade, the humerus which is the upper arm bone and the clavicle or collarbone—''

''Spare me the medical lecture,'' he said, interrupting her, not even attempting to hide his impatience.

Okay, now her aggravation was really reaching dangerous levels. She felt as if she were in a boxing ring. Aggravation versus attraction. In this corner was aggravation—with a stubborn Marine who hated showing any sign of weakness, be it physical or emotional. And in the opposite corner was attraction—to a man who made her hormones zing and her heart sing.

Attraction and aggravation. Together they created a one-two punch that was bound to knock out even the most self-disciplined woman. Combine that with Justice's awesome blue eyes and a mouth to die for and you had a pretty potent package, all wrapped up in a lean, dangerously male body.

So he didn't want a medical lecture? Fine. She wouldn't speak to him at all for the rest of the day. What's more, she wouldn't even tell him she wasn't speaking to him. She'd just go ahead and kill him with silence.

It did occur to her briefly that this was a man who adored silence, but by then she'd already mentally committed to this course of action. Turning on her heel, she walked out of the beach house and left him to stew in his own juices.

The stray dog was waiting for her on the deck with a sloppy grin. Here was someone who liked her, someone who accepted her without question, someone who listened and cared what she thought. So what if his ears were too big for his head, if his paws were out of proportion with his body, if said body could use a good wash....

Twenty minutes later Kelly had hauled a metal washtub from the side of the beach house and filled it with water from the hose she'd attached to an outside faucet. She was going to wash the dog. She was going to accomplish something. The very idea made her feel good.

The dog didn't appear to be equally enamored with the plan, eyeing the metal washtub with Justice-like wariness.

"Don't even go there," Kelly warned the animal. "I don't want to see any of that male distrust on your face. I've had enough of that for one lifetime. I'm not going to drown you in a foot of water, okay? Just get in."

The dog sighed and cautiously moved forward. Of course, the fact that Kelly was holding a doggie treat in her hand might have been a big motivating factor. She'd tossed them in with the groceries when she and Justice had visited the small store yesterday. She still had no idea why the interaction with the people there had so disturbed Justice. He refused to talk about it.

Kelly figured it had something to do with them calling him a hero. Was the guy just being modest? She didn't think so. Justice appeared to have plenty of self-confidence. So why would being called a hero bother him so much? What was the big deal here?

It was a mystery to her, as was Justice. And it looked like he'd remain that way. The frustrating thing was that every so often she'd see a flash of the man behind the iron wall, the man who would smile at her humor, the man who would admire a stunning sunset, the man who kissed with a sensitivity and passion that was beyond description.

Yet he'd only let her get so close before pushing her away. It was incredibly frustrating.

At least the dog was behaving himself, sitting docilely in the metal tub while she soaped him up with a bar of soap she'd filched from the bathroom. Water sloshed over her bare legs and her denim cutoffs but she didn't care.

"What a good baby you are," she crooned as she gently lathered the dog's back. Although he'd fattened up some, she could still feel his spiny backbone, poor thing. "You're being so patient, sitting there. Because you know I'm only trying to help you, right? Unlike that big bad Marine in there, who doesn't have a clue. He doesn't trust anyone, but you trust me don't you, boy?"

The dog licked her cheek.

"I have to come up with a name for you, besides 'The Aforementioned Canine.' Justice calls you that to keep you at a distance, you know. So you shouldn't take it personally. He treats everyone that way. Keeping them at a distance. Only, sometimes you get a flash of the man beneath the tough exterior and that's when you get in trouble."

The dog whined.

"Not that you'd be any trouble. You're so good."

He stood and wagged his tail, almost whacking her across the face with his wet tail. "Hold on, we're not done yet."

The dog sat again, splashing soapy water over the side of the metal tub.

"What I meant about trouble is that when I get a flash of the real Justice, I'm tempted into falling for him and I cannot let that happen. I've told myself that a dozen times already. And now I'm telling you, a dog. But you're an especially understanding dog, aren't you, sweetie?" Using her soapy hands, Kelly rubbed the dog's ears. "A very good listener."

Woof.

"Okay, I'm ready to rinse you now. Just stay." Kelly used one hand to reach out and lift the nearby garden hose. "We have to come up with a name for you. How about Chocolate? You're a dark color and you're sweet. Chocolate sounds good. A perfect name for you."

"It's a dumb name."

Justice's voice startled Kelly, making her lose her grip on the dog and arcing the water from the hose…right across Justice's bare chest.

"You did that on purpose," he accused her.

"I did not. Honest. I didn't even know you were there." Kelly certainly hoped Justice hadn't heard her pouring her heart out to Chocolate. "You shouldn't sneak up on people like that. Oh, wait, I forgot for a moment. That's what you do, isn't it. Sneak up on people."

"Only those who have dangerous secrets to hide."

"That counts me out then."

"I'm not so sure about that."

She aimed the hose at him. "*That* time I hit you on purpose."

"Which calls for retaliation."

"Now, Justice, you deserved it." Even as she was speaking, Kelly was backing away from the beach house and hose, trying to get out of range. "You know you did."

"And you don't deserve retaliation?"

"No, I do not. I was minding my own business washing the dog…"

"Minding your own business? Hah! You never mind your own business."

She made a diving leap for the hose, but he got to it first. "This what you were looking for?" he asked, holding up the hose with his good hand, his expression one of false innocence.

"No." She quickly backed up again. "I was merely trying to check on Chocolate."

"Right," Justice scoffed.

"He'll protect me, you know, so you better be careful."

"The aforementioned canine is no match for me."

"I don't know. He's pretty big."

"So now you're insulting my size? Not real smart."

"Go get him Chocolate."

Woof. The dog leaped out of the soapy water and headed directly for…Kelly.

"No, no, not me. Him. Go get him." She pointed to Justice while backing up even further.

Confused, Chocolate sat down.

Justice was not equally immobile, however. He was definitely coming after her.

Kelly turned and ran across the beach in front of them. Justice took off after her. She took a quick peek over her shoulder and that was her downfall. Literally. She stumbled and fell to the soft sand.

Justice stood above her, lord of all he surveyed, staring down at her with masculine smugness. "This is the second time you've thrown yourself at my feet."

A second later Chocolate had knocked Justice off his feet and onto the sand beside Kelly.

"Are you hurt?" she asked Justice in concern, moving closer to hover over his body.

"I do have a terrible ache," he admitted in a deep husky voice that rolled over her skin like black satin.

"Show me where."

"You'll have to come closer."

She did.

"No, even closer than that."

She shifted, her legs becoming entangled with his, her eyes widening as she felt his throbbing arousal against her. Surely Justice wasn't referring to that ache? Surely he wasn't flirting with her. Surely he wasn't cupping the back of her head with his good hand and lowering her mouth to his.

Oh, but he was. And it felt so good. Beyond good. Incredible. She was blanketing his lean body like seaweed on a rock. There was no part of her anatomy that wasn't touching some part of his. Like two parts of a jigsaw puzzle they fitted together in this horizontal position with meant-to-be precision.

Somehow her braid came loose and her hair slipped down to cover them like a silken curtain. His fingers fondled the soft strands, gently combing through them from the crown of her head to her nape, over her ear.

He was lying on his back, not on his side, which

might have hurt his shoulder. She had the presence of mind to notice that much before she was carried away by a tide of forbidden pleasure.

His kiss held some of the teasing lightness of their earlier exchange with the garden hose, along with the now familiar heated passion. How had she survived so long without his kisses? She could stay this way forever. And she might have if Chocolate hadn't interrupted them by prancing into the ocean and then bounding over to them to shake himself off, spraying them with water.

Kelly and Justice broke off their kiss, but she remained perched atop his body, his good arm pinning her tightly against him.

"We have to stop doing this," Justice said without sounding the least bit convincing and without loosening his hold on her.

"So you keep saying."

"I mean it this time."

"Me, too." She couldn't resist, she just had to place a little series of kisses along his stubborn jaw.

"I'm trying to be serious here."

"Me, too." She kissed his chin.

"Stop that."

"Yes, sir." She saluted him, not easy to do from a horizontal position. Of course he had to kiss her for that, but then he sat up.

"Are you okay?" she asked, wanting to make sure his shoulder wasn't hurting him.

"I've still got that ache," he said, his deep voice still husky.

"I've got one, too," she admitted. "And it's all your fault."

This earned a smile. "My fault, huh?"

"Entirely."

"I seem to recall you doing your fair share in the kissing and seducing department."

"Really?" She was very pleased to hear this news. "The seducing department?"

"Why the surprised look? Surely guys have called you seductive before."

"Oh, yeah. Millions of times."

He wasn't buying her mocking reply. "You reacted the same way when I said you were incredibly sexy yesterday."

"And what way is that?"

"Disbelieving."

"Disbelief is your thing, not mine."

"It takes one to know one. You clearly don't believe that you're a sexy, attractive, seductive woman. Why not?"

"Because I'm not that kind of girl."

"What kind? The bad or good kind?"

"The kind that gets the guy," she said bluntly.

"I find that hard to believe."

She couldn't explain because that would mean bringing up her sister's name, and Kelly didn't want to do that at this point. Not when she and Justice seemed to be forging some new kind of path in their relationship here. How could she tell him that once a guy saw Barbie they never treated Kelly the same?

"Are you telling me you haven't had a guy in your life?"

"Oh, there have been several guys. Most of whom viewed me as the girl-next-door, best-buddy kind of friend. And then there was Dave."

"Who's Dave?"

"The man I thought I could have a future with."

"What went wrong?"

Kelly pulled her knees up to her chest and wrapped her arms around them, keeping her gaze fixed on the line between the blue ocean and the blue sky, and away from the blue of Justice's eyes. "He didn't want to be married to the sort of cute girl next door."

"Sort of cute? What kind of description is that?"

"A description of me."

"It's not my description of you."

She turned to face him. "No? Then what is your description of me?" she whispered, half-afraid to hear his answer.

"A woman who is unafraid, who has the strength of mind and the conviction to put up with me at my worst. A woman with caramel hair that catches the sunlight and throws it back, a woman whose smile makes me want her, a woman who smells so good I want to stay close to you every minute of the day."

His words touched her soul as surely as his kisses and embraces did. She couldn't believe her Marine-of-few-words had suddenly become so eloquent. She couldn't believe he was really talking about her.

She was afraid to believe, so she used humor as a shield. "It's really not me that's sexy or seductive, it's my soap."

"It's you," she thought she heard him murmur but couldn't be sure since she leaped to her feet and brushed the sand off her fanny.

She felt as jumpy as a cat on a hot tin roof, not an original analogy but an accurate one. Opening herself up further to Justice would mean being vulnerable in a way she'd never been in her life, a way that had the power to destroy as well as the power to heal. She didn't want to rush this, she wanted to savor the possibilities here.

But how to tell Justice that? She lacked the experience with men, lacked the words. So she simply said, "I better go get dinner started or we'll starve."

Justice stayed on the beach while Kelly scurried off into the beach house. He hadn't planned on kissing her, hadn't planned on telling her what he'd told her, hadn't planned on revealing that much of himself. But Kelly had a way of getting under his skin and through his defenses.

A wet nose against his bare arm warned Justice of the fact that the aforementioned canine had taken up position on the beach beside him.

"Chocolate. What kind of name is that for a canine?" Justice wasn't talking to the dog, he was talking to himself, but the animal didn't seem to know the difference because it turned its head and barked as if in reply.

"She's making you weak," he told the dog. "You're getting used to having her around. More than used to it, you're *depending* on her presence. You can't do that. It makes you vulnerable, makes you weak. When you have nothing to lose, you're at your most powerful. Remember that."

Had Justice been a fanciful man he might almost have thought the dog was looking at him with pity in his eyes, but he wasn't fanciful, he was a Force Recon Marine, and the word *weakness* was not in his vocabulary.

When you have nothing to lose, you're at your most powerful.

"Listen up, aforementioned canine. If you're

smart you'll hightail it out of here on the double.
Before she turns you into a lapdog, ready to do her
every bidding. What kind of life would that be? A
pampered life that would sap your strength away.
Do not give in, do not surrender. Understood?''

Woof.

''Good. Dismissed.''

The dog stood and trotted away into the twilight.

Chapter Eight

Kelly was basking in the sunshine on the deck the next afternoon, enjoying a rare peaceful moment that ended when Justice joined her. The word *peaceful* and Justice simply did not go together. She'd seen him in his shorts and T-shirt many times before, yet he still had the ability to make her heartrate shoot sky-high. She belatedly noticed that he was carrying his cell phone with him.

"My mother insists on talking to you." He handed her the phone as if handing over a loaded gun.

"Hi, Kelly, how's it going?" Mrs. Wilder asked. "Is my son driving you crazy yet?"

"He accomplished that within the first five minutes," Kelly replied with a grin.

"What?" Justice was demanding. "What did I accomplish?"

"He's being his usual noncommunicative self," Mrs. Wilder said. "When I asked him how his physical therapy was going, he said fine. That's it. One word. Not that Marines are ever the most communicative men in the world, but one word is not enough for me. So tell me, how's he doing?''

"He's impatient with his progress, but he is progressing. He has more range of motion with his injured arm.''

Justice shot Kelly an impatient look, one she was coming to know all too well. "Big deal. So I can lift my arm a few inches, it's still pitiful.''

"Not the best patient, is he? I did try and warn you,'' Mrs. Wilder said.

"I know you did.''

"Don't let him get to you,'' the older woman said.

Kelly's heart stopped. Had Mrs. Wilder somehow picked up the fact that Kelly was falling for Justice? Had Kelly somehow let something slip in the tone of her voice? Or even worse, had Justice said something to his mother, asking her to warn Kelly off? When she'd first arrived Kelly had promised Justice she wouldn't fall for him. She'd always been a woman who took promises seriously. She'd honestly tried very hard to stay objective, to keep her emotional distance. That simply hadn't worked.

"I know his frustration and impatience can be hard to deal with,'' Mrs. Wilder continued.

Kelly relaxed. So his mom wasn't talking about Kelly falling for Justice, thank heaven.

She stole a look at him. He was watching her like a hawk, or like his nickname of Eagle, and had no doubt noticed the way she'd tensed up a moment ago because he said, "What's my mother saying to you?''

"She's telling me all your embarrassing childhood stories," Kelly replied with her customary sauciness.

Mrs. Wilder took her cue immediately. "There was the time that Justice spread margarine all over his brother's hair and all over the kitchen wall."

"She's telling you the margarine story, isn't she?" Justice asked with resignation.

"He was a regular Picasso," Mrs. Wilder continued fondly, "making all kinds of creative swirls on the wall."

"Now she's telling you the Picasso stuff," Justice added with a roll of his blue eyes.

"Tell him to go away so we can talk," Mrs. Wilder ordered.

"Your mother says to go away," Kelly dutifully told Justice.

He didn't budge. "No way."

"Tell him to give us five minutes of privacy," the older woman instructed, "or I'll tell you his childhood streaking story complete with photos."

"Don't move," Kelly told Justice with a grin. "If you stay put, your mom has promised to tell me your childhood streaking story."

Justice muttered under his breath and gave Kelly a dark look before reluctantly taking off for the beach.

"Okay," Kelly told Mrs. Wilder. "He's gone. What's up?"

"I'm afraid I let slip about your sister's upcoming marriage." Mrs. Wilder's voice was filled with regret. "I thought you'd already told Justice."

"No." Kelly's heart sank. "I was waiting for the

right moment. And I wasn't entirely sure that he didn't already know.''

"He didn't."

"What did he say?"

"You know Justice. He didn't say anything. I'm sorry, Kelly. I should have taken a page out of my son's book and not said anything, either."

"That's okay. Is that why you wanted to talk to me without Justice overhearing?"

"That and I wanted to get the straight story on his condition without you having to guard your words around him."

"I'll tell you the same thing I told him, that there are no guarantees and that I can't promise a miracle cure. His injuries to his shoulder were very serious and may require surgery at some point in the future. Even then, there's no guarantee that the tendons can be repaired. He thinks the exercises I'm having him do are wimpy compared to what he's used to in the Marine Corps."

"I'm sure they are wimpy compared to what he's been through in the Marine Corps."

"All we can do is take things one day at a time."

"How long can you stay with him?" Mrs. Wilder asked.

"I've got three weeks of vacation time accrued." She watched Justice as he walked along the beach, his figure already a familiar one to her. Simply watching him gave her pleasure. "We'll see how things go after that."

"You've already been there almost a week."

"And he's made progress during that time. Hopefully that will continue."

"Is he still angry that I sent you out there?"

"Not with you, no. Sometimes he still gets aggravated with me." And other times he kisses me until I can't think straight. The wayward thought streaked through Kelly's mind.

The older woman ended their conversation with, "Like I said before, don't let him get to you."

Kelly couldn't tell Mrs. Wilder that it was already too late—Justice had definitely gotten to her, bigtime.

"Tell me again how fooling around in the ocean is going to help my recovery," Justice demanded an hour later.

"We're not fooling around," Kelly replied, although that image certainly was tempting. Visions of her body tangling with his in the surf filled her head in a remake of the classic Deborah Kerr and Burt Lancaster scene from the movie *From Here to Eternity*.

The day had turned downright hot. Kelly was wearing the lemon-yellow, two-piece swimsuit she'd brought with her. Aside from the brilliant color, there was nothing outrageous about her outfit, no skimpy top or thong bottom. Yet she was very aware of her body...because she was very aware of *his* body. He wasn't wearing a thong, either. The wicked thought made her grin. He looked sexy enough in his briefest running shorts. Apparently, he hadn't brought a suit with him, which was probably a good thing. Seeing him in a swimsuit would probably give her cardiac arrest.

During her time at the beach house he'd often gone without a shirt, as he was now, because getting in and out of that piece of clothing was problematic with his injury. He often wore one of his friend Striker's collection of short-sleeved Hawaiian print shirts left open or only partially buttoned. Again, doing up buttons with his left hand was not the easiest of tasks.

Not that Kelly had ever complained about his casual state of undress. She'd simply enjoyed the view. Which was wicked of her, but there you had it. She was only human.

"We're not fooling around," she repeated, as much for her own benefit as for his. "We're working."

"I don't call this work."

"Well, I do, so listen up."

He lifted a dark eyebrow. "I love it when you go all bossy on me."

"You do not."

He grinned and her heart stopped. Wow. Talk about a secret weapon. That grin of his was lethal, transforming his lean features. He'd also forsaken his "secret" stare for an outright visual seduction as his gaze wandered over her body with leisurely appreciation. Her skin burned, and it wasn't caused by the sun.

"You know me too well," he murmured.

Did she? Did she really know him at all? Her heart knew him, knew he was the one man above all others who held the key to her soul. "You're still a man with plenty of secrets."

"Women like a little mystery."

"Oh, so now you're an expert on what women like?"

"You don't think I'm an expert?"

"You show some potential," she allowed, taking more pleasure than she should in teasing him.

"Potential?"

"Yes, but there's always room for improvement."

"Improvement?" he repeated with mock indignation. "Okay, now you've gone too far." He moved toward her.

"I was just kidding." She put her hand out, her fingertips brushing against the warm skin of his bare chest. The resilience of his flesh over the hard ridges of muscles and ribs reminded her yet again that this was a man in excellent shape. A whorl of dark hair tapered in an erotic motif from his chest down his stomach. He wasn't overly hairy, he was just right. And he was right in front of her, gazing down at her with those incredible blue eyes of his, eyes that reflected a sexy gleam she'd never seen in them before.

"You know what happens to women who kid a Force Recon Marine, don't you?" His voice was deep with sensual promise.

She shook her head, unable to speak.

"I didn't think so." He trailed his left index finger down her cheek, past her jaw, and kept going to the hollow at the base of her throat and lower. "We keep that kind of information highly classified." His erotic caress moved to the valley between her breasts. "Only those with special knowledge have access."

"What sort of special knowledge?" Kelly's voice was husky.

"The knowledge to proceed slowly and assess the situation as you go. Sometimes the most direct route isn't the best choice. Sometimes you need to explore the terrain.'' Justice swirled a sensual design along the creamy slope of her right breast. "These things can't be hurried. Wouldn't you agree?''

"Mmmmm.'' She was swept with intense pleasure, his touch inflaming her. Her body recognized his touch and responded to it with wild abandon, forsaking caution. His skin was slightly rough against hers, creating a delightful friction.

"Some things just require extra attention to detail in order not to overlook all aspects of the primary objective.'' He brushed his palm over her sensitized nipples while his thumbs skimmed the full underside of her breasts. The thin, stretchy material of her swimsuit amplified his caresses until she was utterly steeped in passion. "Nothing can be overlooked in order to ensure that the ultimate mission is a success.''

His mission was clearly to make her go up in flames, and he was doing that with erotic precision.

"So are you ready to begin?'' he asked.

"Begin?'' she whispered, lost in the wonder of his touch.

"Begin the water exercises.'' His wicked grin let her know he was testing her.

"Absolutely. I was just waiting for you to finish your demonstration.''

"Was I interrupting your schedule?''

He'd interrupted her heartbeat and breathing, but he probably realized that already. Fine. Two could play at that game. "Yes, you were and I'm going to have to punish you for that.''

His blue eyes gleamed even brighter. "You are?''

"Yes, I am.''

"And what form would this punishment take?"

"Something designed to test your self-discipline."

"A Marine has plenty of self-discipline."

"So I've heard. Let's see if that's true." This time she was the one who put her hands on him. "We're going to have a pop anatomy quiz. The shoulder is made up of three bones." Her fingers glided from the curved tip of his right shoulder over to his left, performing a woman-to-man dance. "What are they called?"

Justice knew what *this* was called—seduction. She was giving as good as she got, tempting him with her touch as he'd just tempted her. And she was doing a fine job of it. He was impressed and aroused. And she...she seemed to be having fun driving him nuts with her soft fingers running helter-skelter over his chest.

He mentally groaned at her use of the bone imagery. He was certainly as hard as one. She'd done that deliberately, the little devil.

"What's wrong?" she prompted with a knowing grin. "Are you finding this too hard for you? Want some help? I'll give you a clue. This—" she leaned forward to feather-kiss his collarbone "—is the clavicle. Want another clue?"

He wanted to peel the top off her lemon-yellow bathing suit and kiss her bare nipples. He wanted to peel the bottom off and sink into her supple warmth. He wanted to make love to her until the oceans ran dry. In that moment he didn't care whose sister she was, he wanted her with a force that made his mouth go dry and his body throb.

Had she planned this? Was seducing him part of

her reason for showing up here on the island? His distrust ran so deep that even passion couldn't completely overcome it.

His training as a Marine had taught him to beware of surprise attacks. He needed to regroup here. "Time for us both to cool off," he declared, using his good hand to tug her under the water with him.

She was still sputtering when he stood once again, shaking the water out of his eyes like that aforementioned canine. The hot sun had taken the chill off the water. One look at her wet swimsuit plastered to her breasts told him this might not have been the wisest course of action. She looked even more seductive now than she had a moment ago.

"You were just dying to get even with me for getting you wet when I gave Chocolate his bath, weren't you?" she accused him.

Justice nodded, preferring she think that than know the truth—that she'd gotten to him so badly he'd panicked.

"All right, enough fun and games," she said. "Let's get to work. The purpose of water exercises is that the water supports your weight and also helps you move your joints." Even as she went into her physical therapist mode, Kelly couldn't help thinking that she and Justice had just moved to a new place in their ongoing relationship, a place filled with possibilities. "The extra buoyancy avoids the pain…"

"A Marine never avoids pain," Justice informed her. "A Marine works through pain."

"And smiles while doing it, right?"

"Right, ma'am." He shot her a smile that made her knees feel like limp lasagna pasta.

"Must make being married to a Marine a challenge." She didn't know what made her say the words but she regretted them as soon as she'd spoken them.

His smile faded. "Affirmative. Marines have a high divorce rate. Women tend not to understand that a Marine's first commitment is to the Corps."

"I would say that depends on the woman," she replied. "Look at your mom and dad. They've been married a long time."

"And it hasn't always been easy."

"I never said it was easy. I'm not into easy."

"Their marriage isn't your typical marriage."

"Then don't settle for 'typical,'" Kelly said. "Wait for 'special' with a woman independent and strong enough that she doesn't have to depend on you being with her every second of the day."

"Women like that don't grow on trees."

No, they don't. But one is standing in front of you, she wanted to shout at him.

As if reading her mind, Justice softly said, "Are you a woman like that? One strong enough to be married to a Marine?"

"Absolutely," Kelly replied. "But then I'm not into 'easy.' I like a challenge."

His smile returned. "I'll keep that in mind."

"You do that." She grinned, feeling as though she and Justice had just turned a corner. She couldn't wait to see where things would go from here.

The next ten days with Justice passed like sand sifting through open fingers, going by in a heartbeat. There was a newfound sense of discovery in every day as she sensed him gradually opening up to her. When she'd first arrived on the island, she'd never have dreamed that Justice would do anything as romantic as suggesting a moonlit walk along the wide beach. But he'd done that tonight.

Of course, being Justice, he was also regaling her with pirate stories. The man clearly related to their nautical recon adventures. "Legend has it that on a foggy night you can look out across the Atlantic from here and see the ghostly silhouette of a pirate's ship as the notorious Blackbeard sails his ship back out to the open ocean. He died in a bloody battle in a nearby inlet."

Looking out at the full moon shimmering on the restless ocean it was all too easy to imagine those bygone days when pirates hid their plunder beneath the palmettos before sailing off.

"What, you're not going to recite some little-known fact about Blackbeard to me?" Justice teased her.

"Who me? No, I don't have anything to add aside from the fact that North Carolina's coast is known as the Graveyard of the Atlantic because of all the sunken ships located here. And the fact that divers recently found what is believed to be Blackbeard's flagship two miles off Beaufort Inlet."

"How do you know that?"

"I read about it somewhere. But that's all I know. I have no other tidbits of information about him to recite to you."

"That's a first."

All of this was a first for her. Her first steps into a new relationship with Justice, one that had her pinching herself in the morning to make sure she wasn't dreaming.

She'd tried to pinpoint exactly what had changed between them. Attraction was no longer fighting with aggravation, having won that battle. Now she and Justice were exploring the new territory of flirtatious interludes like this one tonight.

He placed his good arm around her shoulders as they walked side by side, avoiding the section of beach where the turtles were nesting farther south. The warmth of his body along her right side warmed her soul. This felt so right, so meant-to-be that it was almost frightening.

She'd given up trying to anticipate the future, or worrying about the past, and instead was entirely devoted to living in the moment. Justice made her feel protected, filling her heart with a warm delight that made her want to curl her toes in the sand. She had her arm around his lean waist, matching her stride to his. His shoulder was tempting her to rest her head there.

Temptation was all around her—in the sultry night air, in the magical moonlight, in the hypnotic sound of the waves hitting the shore, and most especially in the sexy man by her side.

She loved him. The realization had come to her gradually, or perhaps the emotions had been there all along, just waiting to resurface when she met him again. She couldn't pinpoint the exact moment when it happened, there hadn't been any single incident that had precipitated the knowledge. She just knew she loved him.

She didn't know what he felt for her. But she did know that she loved the way he looked at her, the way he touched her, the camaraderie as they cooked dinner together, the competitiveness as they played a game of poker, the flirtation they were both indulging in. Except during his therapy sessions. During those they were both focused on his recovery.

Justice continued to make some progress although not at the rate he wanted. She thought he was doing well, which was why his outburst the next afternoon caught her entirely by surprise.

"I hate this!" He tossed the foam ball he'd been using across the living room. "This is a waste of time." His voice vibrated with pent-up frustration. "I'm no closer to rejoining my squad now than I was when you got here."

"Your range of motion has improved…."

"From useless to pitiful, big deal."

"It's not pitiful unless you make it that way. Are you still sleeping on your left side to avoid the pain…"

"I told you before, a Marine doesn't avoid pain," Justice shot back curtly. "He works through it."

"Sometimes that's not always possible."

A muscle clenched in his jaw. "My C.O. called me this morning. Checking in on my progress, he said. Telling me my squad was shipping out without me under a new command. I've been replaced."

"Oh, Justice, I'm so sorry…"

"I don't want your pity," he said fiercely.

His blue eyes were so stark they seemed to blaze across the room. Anger tightened the skin on his lean cheeks and compressed his lips into a grim line.

Her heart ached for him. "Why didn't you tell me earlier?"

"Why? What good would it have done? I'll never

be the man I once was. What's the point of any of this if I can't get my life back?"

"It doesn't change the man you are inside. A heroic man who saved the life of a child regardless of the danger to himself."

His face became even bleaker. "I'm no hero."

"I know you keep saying that…"

"Because it's true." He sank onto the couch and buried his face in his hands.

She knelt beside him. "Justice…"

He raised his head, gazing at her with anguish. "You don't know what it's like."

"What what's like?"

"Being hailed a hero, when deep down a part of me…" his voice faltered. "A part of me wonders if I would have saved that child knowing it would mean giving up my life with Force Recon."

"Oh, Justice." Kelly wrapped her arms around his broad shoulders. "You are a hero, but you're also human. It's natural to have those thoughts. But the bottom line is that you would have helped that child no matter what, because that's the type of man you are."

"You can't know that."

"Yes, I can. And I *do* know that. Honor, courage, commitment. It's ingrained in you. Bone deep. Do you regret what happened, what you've lost? Absolutely. And that's okay. Yes, you're a Marine and, yes, you might not get your old life back exactly as it was before, but this is a rare chance for you to start a new life filled with new opportunities in the Marine Corps."

"As some flunkie paper pusher? No, thanks."

"You're a Force Recon Marine, Justice. I think

you can come up with a more creative use of your talents than becoming a paper pusher. Someone has to train the next generation of Force Recon recruits. Why couldn't it be you? And before you go telling me that you can't do what you did before, let me remind you that there's more than one way to teach, you don't have to show them how to do it, you can tell them, let them learn from your experience. Remember, a Marine never gives up, no excuses, no exceptions.''

''No excuses, no exceptions,'' he repeated, cupping her face with his good hand. He lowered his lips to hers so slowly that she felt them coming before they touched and parted her own. His tongue sought admission and she quickly granted him access. He rewarded her with tantalizing thrusts, creating a heated exchange that made her melt against him.

Hauling her closer with his good arm, he draped her across his lap. The chemistry that had been building between them for the past few weeks now flared totally out of control. Walls tumbled down as they reached for each other with raw intensity.

Kelly had never felt closer to him. Finally he'd let her get a glimpse into his heart, into the darkness he'd guarded so well. No wonder he'd reacted the way he had when they'd gone to the local store and they'd called him a hero. These doubts had been eating away at him all this time and he'd never let her know, never confided in her. Until now.

Now was all that mattered. She felt the warmth of his lips traveling down her jaw and throat to the open vee of her shirt. When he growled at the uselessness of his right hand in undoing her buttons, she undid them for him, undoing his while she was at it. Now there was nothing but the silkiness of her bra separating her breasts from his chest. The warmth of his skin heated her even further, making her burn with desire.

Justice shifted, lowering her onto the couch beneath him. She felt his arousal pressing against her as her legs tangled with his. Striving to get closer, she arched against him. Murmuring unintelligible words of seduction, Justice lowered his mouth to her bra, paying homage to her nipples with a tongue still warm and wet from their kiss. Her fingers slid through his dark hair before closing convulsively and tugging his head closer. The bra's delicate front fastener soon gave way, freeing her breasts. He celebrated her newfound freedom by closing his lips around her and tugging her nipple gently, sweetly into his mouth.

Ecstasy. Hot, addictive. Ripples of pleasure surged deep within her. Each delicious movement he made created another level of fierce delight. She gasped, lost in the feverish exhilaration.

More. She wanted more.

As if reading her mind, he shifted his attention to her other breast. *Yes, yes, yes!* She writhed against him, the liquid ache driving her toward him. He moved against her, creating a friction between them that made her crazy.

Her hands slid down his bare chest to his waist. Their clothing was getting in the way. She wanted it gone. But that would mean moving away from him and she couldn't bear to do that. So she instead shoved his shirt off his broad shoulders and showered him with kisses wherever she could reach.

He responded by cupping his good hand around her breast and shifting his mouth back up her body. Her mouth was vulnerable and invitingly open as she welcomed his returning kiss.

The world slipped away as her attention was utterly focused on Justice, on the man she loved. Passion seemed to vibrate from the very heart of him, catching her up in an erotic riptide from which she never wanted to escape.

This was it. This was what she'd been waiting for her entire life. She'd never felt this way about another man before. Her experience with Dave paled in comparison to what she was experiencing now with Justice.

"Make love to me," she whispered against his mouth.

His blue eyes flared with passion as he gazed down at her for a heartbeat before kissing her again, holding nothing back.

The pounding sound she first attributed to her own thundering heart was quickly followed by a high-pitched feminine screech. "What do you think you're doing to my little sister?"

Kelly's eyes flew open to find Barbie standing over them like an avenging goddess.

Chapter Nine

"**B**arbie!" Kelly hastily gathered her shirt together, trying to cover her bare breasts. "What are you doing here?"

"What am *I* doing?" her sister practically shrieked. "What are *you* doing?"

"Did you tell her to come here?" Justice demanded, sitting up and eyeing both women with the suspicion Kelly knew all too well. "Is this some kind of a setup?"

"Setup?" Barbie repeated. "You're the one who's setting up my poor baby sister."

"I did not tell her to come here," Kelly quickly assured Justice. She scrambled to an upright position, frantically trying to think of a way to refasten her bra without drawing further attention to the fact it was still undone. "I didn't even tell her where I was."

"Of course she didn't. If she had I would never have allowed her to come out here to this godforsaken place," Barbie stated, looking around with disdain. She was perfectly dressed, without one spot of sand or dust marring her white pantsuit. Her designer spectator pumps cost more than Kelly made in a month and her haircut didn't leave one blond strand out of place. A huge diamond flashed on her left hand. The coral silk blouse she wore matched the coral and gold necklace around her neck.

In comparison Kelly just noticed her own shirt was buttoned lopsidedly while Justice hadn't bothered buttoning his at all.

"You don't like this godforsaken place, then leave. You've got no business being here," Justice told Barbie, his jaw clenched in anger.

"No business? My sister is my business."

"How did you find me?" Kelly asked, attempting to prevent Justice and Barbie from any further fighting, even though she knew that was probably a hopeless cause.

"I dropped by your town house in Nashville and your neighbor told me you were treating your sister's ex-husband on some deserted island."

Kelly cursed herself for giving her neighbor that much information. But she'd had to tell someone where she was going, and her neighbor was taking in her mail for her and watering her houseplants while she was gone.

"Daddy is not pleased, either," Barbie added.

"You told our father?" Her voice reflected her dismay.

"Of course I did. He's on business in California or he would have come out here himself." Barbie shifted her gorgeous blue eyes from Kelly to the man beside her. "I can't believe you've sunk this low, Justice."

"And how low is that, Barbie?" he shot back.

"Trying to get back at me by seducing my sister."

Kelly sputtered. "He didn't...he wasn't..." She couldn't even get the words out. "Tell her, Justice."

"Yes, tell me, Justice," Barbie drawled with her perfect Southern lady accent. "Swear on your honor as a Marine that you weren't out for a little revenge here."

Kelly waited for him to do so. She waited in vain.

"Justice?" Her voice was uncertain.

"I don't have to swear anything. The days of you ordering me around are long gone," Justice told Barbie.

"Just tell her it isn't true," Kelly said. "Please, Justice. Tell her it isn't true."

Silence.

"He can't," Barbie said. "Because it *is* true."

No. No. It couldn't be true. Justice wouldn't have done something that cruel. Would he?

He would if his anger at Barbie went deep enough.

Memories came tumbling back as Kelly replayed the conversation with Mrs. Wilder in her head. *I told him about Barbie's engagement.* That had been the day they'd started water therapy in the ocean, the day Justice had taken his flirting to a new level.

He'd never mentioned Barbie's engagement, never given Kelly any indication of his reaction to the news. She should have asked him, but she'd been distracted.

And then there was that bitter comment he'd

made the first day she'd arrived: *Haven't you Hart women messed up my life enough already?*

Revenge. Was that all that motivated Justice? Had he merely used Kelly as an instrument to get back at Barbie? Was he yet another man not seeing her for herself?

She stared at Justice's tightly controlled features, willing him to say something to make matters right, hoping against hope that she'd see something in his eyes that would make her believe…

But there was nothing there aside from anger at Barbie. And beneath that…a flash of guilt.

Kelly's breath caught as pain rammed into her with the force of a tidal wave. It was true. There was no other reason Justice wouldn't deny it, no reason at all. She hadn't expected him to bare his soul, but she'd never anticipated that he'd just stand there without saying a word in his own defense.

He couldn't swear on his honor as a Marine that he hadn't used her, because it was true. He had used her to get back at Barbie. Kelly cringed at how easy she'd made it for him, how quickly she'd fallen for him.

"Was that your plan?" Kelly demanded. "To seduce me? And what, then go tell Barbie about it?"

"There was no plan…" Justice finally said.

"How unlike a Marine," Kelly angrily interrupted him. "I thought you always went into battle with a plan. And this was a battle all along, wasn't it? A battle between you and my sister."

Kelly had studied anatomy, she knew that medically speaking a heart couldn't actually shatter and break. But it sure felt that way to her, as if her heart was shattering into tiny pieces.

She couldn't fall apart here. She was the one who always managed, the one who could handle anything. Except this.

"I don't want to settle for a man who is still hung up on my sister." The words were out of Kelly's mouth before she could stop them.

"You don't have to *settle* at all," Justice replied, obviously stung by her use of that word.

"No, I don't," Kelly said quietly. "And I don't have to stay here, either."

"That's right," Barbie said, coming to her side. "I've got a boat waiting to take us back to the mainland. Pack up your stuff and we'll get out of here."

"It won't take me long." Kelly had already refastened her shirt and was stuffing her remaining clothing into her backpack with lightning speed. She ignored the trembling of her fingers, blocked out the churning in her stomach and held on to her anger to see her through the utter misery.

"So much for your fancy words about not abandoning those you love," Justice said. "Sticking like glue was the way you put it."

"I never said I love you," Kelly shot back, grateful that she hadn't exposed herself to that extent.

"I was referring to the aforementioned canine." Justice pointed to the still-open front door where Chocolate sat looking at Kelly with forlorn eyes.

"I'm not leaving Chocolate," Kelly stated. "I'm taking him with me."

Barbie eyed the animal with dismay.

Gathering up her backpack, Kelly turned to face Justice. "I'll fax your physician a written report on your physical therapy."

"Don't bother."

She ignored his words. "You should continue the exercises and return for another medical evaluation. I've helped you all I can, the rest is up to you," she told him before leaving with her sister and the afore-mentioned canine.

Justice stared at the door, telling himself he was well rid of those Hart women, telling himself that Kelly shouldn't have believed her sister, telling himself that he didn't have to answer to Barbie. And in between telling himself all that, Justice was also wondering…wondering how things could have gone so wrong so quickly.

An hour later Justice was out on the deck, nursing a cold beer, when he heard the front door open. Adrenaline rushed through his system, filling the gaping hole caused by Kelly's departure. Leaping to his feet, he rushed inside.

"I knew you'd come back…" Justice began, and then stopped when he realized it wasn't Kelly but his buddy Striker who stood in the doorway.

"Of course I came back. I live here." Striker dumped a duffle bag on the floor. At the moment he looked more like a surfer than a Marine with his dark tan, khaki shorts and outrageous Hawaiian shirt in neon yellow and lime. "You were expecting someone else?"

"Not really."

"So you've developed some sort of ESP that lets you know someone's whereabouts?" his buddy mocked him. "That kind of talent could come in real handy for a Force Recon Marine."

"My C.O. called this morning and told me that my squad shipped out without me."

"Yeah, I heard. That stinks."

"Is that why you're here?"

"Nah, I came to do a little fishing."

"Yeah, right." Justice's throat tightened with emotion. Striker was a loyal friend. But guys didn't talk about junk like that.

Emotions had always been a land mine to be avoided as far as Justice was concerned. His divorce had only reaffirmed that tendency. And his work with Force Recon made him doubt people's motives, question their actions.

He'd been sitting out on the deck reviewing what had happened over and over again. What if the something he'd sensed Kelly had been hiding from him all along was the fact that she had a thing for him?

Yes, she'd told him that overbearing Marines weren't her type. But she wasn't the type of woman to let him get that intimate with her otherwise.

They'd almost made love, would have made love if his ex-wife hadn't stormed in on them.

Kelly had promised him that she wouldn't go all goofy over him, but what if she hadn't been able to keep that promise? He'd promised himself that he wouldn't get involved with her, and he'd certainly broken that promise.

Kelly loved him. He tested that theory like someone testing a new filling after going to the dentist. He needed to talk to her, he needed to find out if it was true.

"So how's it going here?" Striker asked.

"Did you happen to see a woman with caramel-colored wavy hair getting into a boat down at the dock?" Justice casually asked.

"I saw a skinny blonde in a white pantsuit."

"My ex-wife."

"A real looker, but seems very high maintenance."

Justice nodded. "You've got that right."

"So why are you interested in the other woman?"

"I'm not interested, I was just wondering. She was my physical therapist."

"And she took off with your ex-wife?" Striker raised an eyebrow. "What's that about?"

"She's also my ex-wife's younger sister."

Striker shook his head. "Jeez, Wilder, that could get messy."

"It did."

"So what happened? The ex-wife walk in on you and her sister?" Seeing the look on Justice's face, Striker said, "That's it, isn't it? So I missed the catfight?"

"There was no catfight."

"Too bad." Striker hooked a beer from the fridge with one hand and grabbed a bag of chips with his other on his way out to the back deck. Stopping in his tracks, he returned to the fridge. "Is that homemade lasagna I see in here?"

"Yeah. How did you know it's homemade?"

"Because frozen doesn't look or smell like this." Striker lifted the plastic wrap and closed his eyes in ecstasy as he ate the first bite with a fork. "Who is responsible for this delicious dish?"

"You're eating it cold, how can it be delicious?"

"As you know, I've eaten beetles and snakes when the situation warrants it. Believe me this is delicious. Want some?"

Justice shook his head. His stomach was in knots. "I know what it tastes like."

"And you don't think it's great? I had no idea that Earl sold anything in his tiny store that could be turned into this heavenly dish."

"She brought the stuff with her."

Striker took another bite. "She who? Who made it? Give me her name so I can marry her immediately."

"Forget it."

"Oh, so you want to keep her for yourself, huh? I can understand that. I wouldn't share if I were you, either. Does she live here on the island?"

"No, she took off in a boat with my ex-wife."

"You mean your physical therapist made this for you? Man, I've clearly been going to the wrong hospitals." Striker dropped the bag of chips and instead grabbed the entire pan of lasagna before going to the deck. "So what's this girl's name?"

"She's not a girl. She's a woman."

Striker paused. "Uh-oh."

"Uh-oh?" Justice repeated in irritation. "What's that supposed to mean?"

"I leave you alone for three weeks and you go and fall for a woman." Striker sadly shook his head. "I expected better of you, buddy."

"I did not fall in love with Kelly!" Justice growled.

"Oh, so that's her name. I like it. And her lasagna." Striker took another bite along with a sip of his beer. "Caramel-colored wavy hair, you say? Yeah, now that I think on it, I do recall seeing her on the dock. Long sexy hair, big brown eyes, legs to die for, and she was toting a big dog."

"So she did take the aforementioned canine."

"A woman who cooks like an angel, looks great and likes dogs. Sounds like heaven to me. If you don't marry her, I will."

"Stop saying that."

"Why do you care?"

"I don't."

Striker didn't say a word, just gave him a look.

Justice relented. "Okay, so maybe she did get to me a little...."

Striker's gaze didn't waver one iota.

"I'm no good at love," Justice bit out. "Especially not with my ex-wife's sister."

"Too hard for you, huh? Still stuck on your ex?"

"No way."

"Then what's the problem? How does she feel about you? Was Kelly just out for a fast roll in the sack with a Marine? Was that the problem? If so, I can oblige her with that—"

The words were barely out of Striker's mouth when Justice grabbed his colorful shirtfront. "Take that back! Kelly isn't like that."

Striker just grinned at him. "Yep, you're in love. I can see why that would scare you spitless."

"I'm a Marine," Justice ground the words out between clenched teeth. "We don't scare easy."

"Not easy, no. But love, man, that's a dangerous thing. Plenty to be scared about there. Especially for us Marines."

Justice slowly released his buddy's shirt and sank onto a nearby canvas deck chair.

"I take it from that stupefied look on your face, that it's finally occurred to you what's wrong with you," Striker said.

"She got to me, that's all," Justice muttered. "Got under my skin."

Striker nodded. "I hear that's one of the symptoms. Grabbing your best friend and threatening him bodily harm over a woman is another sure sign."

Justice swore.

"Whatever you want to call it, it's love, buddy. And you've got my deepest sympathy," Striker added. "I wouldn't want to be in your shoes for anything in the world."

"So what do I do now?"

"If you want her, go after her."

"I don't even know where she lives in Nashville. But my mother does."

"Your mother?" Striker repeated in disbelief. "What does your mother have to do with this?"

"I'll explain later." Justice grabbed his cell phone and called home.

"Justice, it's so good to hear from you," his mom said, her voice reflecting her pleasure.

Never one to beat around the bush, Justice said, "Mom, what's Kelly's phone number and address in Nashville?"

He should have known his mother wouldn't make it easy for him. "Why don't you ask her?"

"Because she's not here right now."

"Where is she?"

"I don't know," he replied.

"You don't know?" his mom repeated suspiciously. "What did you do?"

"What makes you think I did anything?"

"Because Kelly wouldn't have left that island early unless you drove her away. What did you do?"

"I can't go into it right now..." Justice began when she interrupted him.

"Then I can't give you Kelly's phone number."

"Fine. I'll call information."

"She has an unlisted number. But I don't, which is how Kelly's father was able to reach me about ten minutes ago. Care to tell me how he found out that Kelly was there with you?"

Justice sighed. "Barbie told him."

"How did Barbie find out?"

"It's a long story, Mom. Look, just give me Kelly's number. I have to talk to her."

Striker grabbed the phone from him and shouted into it, "The poor sap is totally besotted with Kelly." He then handed the phone back to Justice.

"Who was that?" Mrs. Wilder demanded.

"My ex-buddy Striker." Justice glared at him.

"Is what he said true? Is that why you want Kelly's phone number? Because you love her?"

Justice tried not to squirm. Jeez, this was his idea of torture, having to confess his emotions. He'd rather have bamboo shoots stuck under his fingernails. He'd rather eat ground glass and beetles. He'd rather walk over hot coals.

"Is Dad around?" he asked somewhat desperately.

"Your father is playing golf. Or trying to." She sighed before relenting. "If I do give you Kelly's number, you have to swear to me that you won't hurt her again."

"What do you mean *again?*" he said defensively.

"I mean she wouldn't have left in the first place if you hadn't hurt her. Don't do it again, Justice. Or you'll have to answer to me. Are we clear on that?"

"Affirmative." He quickly scribbled down the information she gave him.

"And, Justice, before you get to Nashville, I suggest you practice your speech."

He frowned. "What speech is that?"

"The one that will convince Kelly to let you back into her life."

Chapter Ten

"I can't believe you brought that mangy dog with you. Look what he's done to my pantsuit," Barbie demanded as they stood in the marina parking lot. The boat ride back to the mainland had been fast and uneventful, aside from the fact that Chocolate kept wanting to jump ship.

Kelly had focused her attention on keeping the dog onboard, which prevented her from paying attention to her sister's nonstop complaints. It also prevented her from thinking about Justice and the way he hadn't even bothered denying Barbie's accusation. The thing was, he hadn't just kept quiet— for a brief second Kelly had seen a flash of guilt in his eyes before he'd shut down and emotionally removed himself from the situation.

Not that he really had removed himself because, after all, he had seemed completely capable of expressing his anger at his ex-wife. Kelly wondered what had ever made her think that she could erase the memories of their relationship from Justice's mind. She couldn't. He was firmly entrenched in the love-hate thing he had going with Barbie, so much so that he'd used Kelly as a way of striking back at Barbie.

Kelly had known she was walking into a hornet's nest when she'd answered Mrs. Wilder's call for help. She'd seen the dangers, and yet that hadn't prevented her from falling for Justice all over again. Only this time she wasn't a naive thirteen-year-old with a crush on her older sister's boyfriend; this time she was a woman in love with the wrong man.

Pain vied with humiliation to get the upper hand but she couldn't afford to give in to either one right now. Kelly told herself she wasn't the first woman to make a mistake and she wouldn't be the last.

"I never thought I'd see the day when conservative Justice would wear a Hawaiian shirt," Barbie was saying.

"It wasn't his. The shirt belongs to his friend who owns the beach house. Justice's shoulder injury made wearing shirts easier than wearing his usual T-shirts." Unemotional words, nothing there to make Kelly cry. But the tears came, anyway, out of the blue but from the depths of her broken heart.

"Are you crying?" Barbie asked in astonishment. "You are! I don't understand. You never cry. Not even when Mother died."

"I cried inside," Kelly whispered, wiping away the tears with an angry swipe of her hand. But they kept coming, faster than she could wipe them away. Dropping to her knees, she hugged Chocolate, burying her face in his fur as the sobs started coming in earnest.

"There, now..." Her sister sounded completely at a loss. "There's no need for a scene. I can buy another suit, you don't have to feel bad about your dog ruining this one."

Kelly leaned away from Chocolate to stare up at Barbie as if seeing her for the first time. "It's always about you, isn't it?"

"This is the thanks I get for coming to your rescue? Think what might have happened if I hadn't walked in when I had."

"I know what would have happened," Kelly angrily replied, fed up with her sister's constant self-involvement. "Justice and I would have made love. That's what I wanted to happen."

"He seduced you...."

"I seduced him more than he seduced me."

Barbie's mouth dropped open before she looked around in dismay. "We are not having a personal conversation like this in the middle of a public parking lot," she whispered. "I rented a room at a resort nearby." She named a well-known hotel. "I'll drive us there and we can sit down and have a nice chat."

Yes, Kelly decided, it was time she and her sister had a talk. "I'll drive myself and meet you there."

Barbie eyed her uncertainly. "Promise me you won't take off. Promise me you'll meet me at the resort?"

"I promise."

"Cross you heart and hope to die?"

Kelly stared at her sister in surprise. "You haven't said that since we were kids."

"Cross your heart," Barbie ordered.

"Fine. I cross my heart."

"It doesn't count if you don't make the motion with your right index finger when you say it."

"Oh for heaven's sake. I cross my heart." Kelly made the sign of an *X* over her heart as she spoke.

"You have to say what you promise before you cross your heart."

Kelly narrowed her eyes at her. "Now you're starting to aggravate me." Actually, her sister had started doing that the moment they'd stepped into the boat back on the island.

Barbie apparently decided she'd pushed Kelly far enough because she backed down. "Okay, I'll see you there. It's only four miles down the main road, to the left."

Kelly watched her sister drive away before moving toward her own car, which she'd left in the lot almost three weeks ago when she'd first come to see Justice. So much had changed in that time.

Woof.

"For one thing I'm a dog owner, now," Kelly said, determined not to dissolve into tears again. She stopped at the marina store and got some bottled water for Chocolate as well as some beef jerky. They didn't sell dog food. The clerk offered her a used leash and collar.

"My boyfriend left them behind in my car when he took off with our dog," the girl told Kelly. "Men are the ticks on pond scum."

"Yes, they are," Kelly agreed.

"I've been meaning to get rid of the dog stuff. Go ahead and take it."

Kelly did. Chocolate wasn't thrilled at the idea of being leashed, but she didn't want him running away. She offered the dog a stick of beef jerky as a reward.

"That will have to hold you over until I can stop at a grocery store. Right after I talk to Barbie, we'll get your food and then head home to Nashville. You'll like it there. No stubborn Marines within fifty miles of my town house."

Despite the hot sun beating down on her, Kelly felt cold inside, as if she'd stashed her emotion on ice. Which was something Justice would have done. Emotions just get in the way, he'd told her. He was right. She should have taken a page out of his book and not let her emotions rule her head.

She felt like such an idiot. She'd been wrapped up in the possibilities of a future with Justice. To give him credit, he'd never lied to her and promised her anything. Not with words, maybe. But he'd promised plenty with those addictive kisses of his.

What would she have done if Barbie had come a day later? What if Kelly and Justice had already made love? Would that have changed anything? Or would his betrayal only have been deeper?

It all made sense now, his interest in her, his increasing passion after finding out about Barbie's upcoming nuptials. Kelly had been too besotted to figure things out. She wasn't the kind of woman to inspire passion in a man, especially a man like Justice. She should have figured something was going on. But he'd made her believe...

"Men are the ticks on pond scum," Kelly repeated. "I need to stay angry at him," she told Chocolate. "Otherwise I'll start crying again. And neither one of us wants that, right? I can't drive if I'm crying. So no crying, okay? That's the rule."

She wiped away an errant tear and bit her lip. "No crying," she whispered, closing her eyes. "Absolutely not. No way. No crying. And no loving a man who still loves my sister."

"What do you mean there are no more boats going to the mainland today?" Justice demanded at the ferry office. "I need to get off this island."

"Sorry," the wrinkled scarecrow of a man in charge of things said. His red plastic name tag proclaimed his name was Ned. "You'll have to wait until tomorrow."

"But the schedule says the last ferry doesn't leave until five and it's only four now."

Ned shrugged his bony shoulders. "It left early."

Justice ground his teeth. "What if I had a medical emergency?"

"Then Marge would phone in a request for a helicopter rescue. But only Marge can do that."

"Surely there must be someone with a power boat who'd be willing to take me to the mainland."

"Is there a problem?" It was Marge or, as Justice called her, the turtle lady.

"This guy wants to get back to the mainland," Ned replied. "I told him the ferry left already."

"And there's a Neptune's Folly boat race today, so you won't find many sailors or fishermen around," Marge told Justice. "They're all over on the other side of the island, at the marina with Earl. That's where the race takes place. Well away from the turtle nesting area. Why do you need to get to the mainland today?"

"It's personal."

"Where's Kelly?" Marge looked around as if expecting her to appear.

"She's on the mainland," Justice said curtly. "That's why I need to get there."

"You had a fight?"

What was this? An interrogation? All he needed was a damn boat and someone to skipper it.

Seeing his frown, Marge said, "I'm sorry I can't help you but I don't have a boat. If you went over to Earl's, you might find someone there willing to help you out."

Justice shuddered. Returning to that marina was the last thing he wanted to do. The last time he'd been there he'd almost choked over them all hailing him as a hero. Going back would mean facing that again.

Confessing his inner fears to Kelly had been what had gotten him into trouble in the first place today. Well, maybe not. Maybe letting down his defenses had been the smartest thing he'd ever done. The dumbest might have been ever considering using Kelly for revenge against Barbie, even for a brief moment.

"Do you know the way to Earl's?" Marge asked.

"I know the way."

It was one of the longest walks Justice had ever taken. And his spirits didn't lift any when Earl hailed him with the greeting, "Hey, it's the Marine hero!"

"I ordered us some tea from room service," Barbie said. "I don't think the management approves of dogs in the room, though."

"I couldn't leave Chocolate in the car, it's too

hot. The temperature in a car can reach over 160 degrees within ten minutes this time of year."

"How do you know things like that? You always had statistics and figures like that at your finger-tips."

Kelly remembered Justice teasing her just a few brief days ago, when he'd been regaling her with pirate ghost stories. *What, you're not going to recite some little-known fact about Blackbeard to me?*

She wouldn't be reciting anything to Justice ever again, and that knowledge was like a blade slicing through her soul.

"I just hope no one saw you sneak the dog in through the patio," Barbie was saying even as she poured herself a cup of tea, leaving Kelly to help herself. "It's lucky I have a room on the first floor. Anyway, enough about the dog. I've got so much to tell you about the wedding. It's only in a few months now and I've finally decided on the caterer. They do all the big names in Atlanta. By the way, the dressmaker told me that you haven't stopped by for your fitting for your bridesmaid dress. I specifically got that dressmaker in Nashville to help with your dress so that you'd be able to do the fittings."

Kelly returned her cup to the saucer with a de-cided clink. "I can't believe you're sitting there calmly talking about your wedding after what I've been through today."

Barbie stared at her if she'd grown two heads. "I've never heard you talk that way to me before."

"Well, maybe I should have. Why did you come to the island today? Because I missed a dress fitting for your wedding?"

"Because I was worried about you," Barbie said

quietly. "You've always been the dependable one, the reliable one. I knew something had to have gone wrong for you not to make that appointment. I tried calling you but got no answer."

"Dad could have told you that I was vacationing with a friend."

"He did tell me. But that didn't sound like you."

Kelly frowned. "What do you mean?"

"You've never taken a three-week vacation in your life."

"So you went all the way from Atlanta to my town house in Nashville because you didn't believe I'd taken a three-week vacation?"

"I was in Nashville with my fiancé, who was there on business. While I was there I thought I'd drop by your place to see if you were back yet and just not answering your phone or something. It's just a feeling I had, okay? A feeling that you needed me. And you did."

"I needed you after our mother died, but you didn't help me then."

Barbie was clearly startled by Kelly's husky confession. "You were always the tough one. I thought you were fine."

"I wasn't. I wouldn't have gotten through that time without the help of Mrs. Wilder."

"Justice's mom?"

Kelly nodded. "We've continued to keep in touch over the years. In fact, we've become friends, good friends. I never told you or Dad because I didn't think you'd understand. She called me when Justice was injured and asked for my help. I'd do anything for Mrs. Wilder. She was there when I needed her."

"When I wasn't," Barbie said quietly. "So this

is all my fault. If I'd been a better sister to you after Mother died then you wouldn't have had to rely on Mrs. Wilder and you wouldn't have been called out to the island with Justice.''

''It isn't a matter of whose fault it is. I'm an adult. I was afraid Justice might still be harboring some feelings for you, but I fell in love with him, anyway.''

''Oh, Kelly.''

''Yeah, I know. Stupid, huh? Expecting him to see me after being with you. You'd think I'd learn. I mean I've had a lifetime to get used to it.''

''Used to what?''

''To you being number one. First with Dad, then with Dave and always with Justice.''

''Hold on a minute,'' Barbie protested, waving her perfectly manicured hand in the air. ''I didn't do anything with Dave.''

''You don't have to do anything, you just have to be around a guy and they are your slaves.''

''Oh, please.'' Barbie rolled her eyes in a movement more akin to something Kelly would do. ''You think a guy never dumped me? Plenty of them have, starting with Justice.''

''But you said you divorced him and that's why he wanted revenge against you.''

''I did divorce him, but Justice had left me emotionally before that. He just hates to lose, so he didn't want to admit our relationship was over. As for Dad, he's always bragging about how smart you are to anyone and everyone who'll listen.''

''Only because I'm not beautiful like you.''

''And I'm not smart like you. You're the sister with her act together, not me. The truth is, deep down, you've sort of intimidated me because of your ability to manage, no matter what.''

"You're kidding, right?" Kelly said.

"No, I'm serious."

"You never said anything like this before."

"Well, neither have you." Barbie set down her teacup and sat beside Kelly on the bed. "I admit I may be a bit self-absorbed, but I do care about you, you know."

A second later Kelly and her sister were hugging each other and crying while Chocolate stared up at them as if they were aliens from another planet.

"I guess we have Justice to thank for bringing us a little closer together," Barbie said with a small laugh.

"Yeah, we have Justice to thank for that," Kelly agreed. And for breaking my heart, she silently added. Breaking it beyond repair.

"Thanks for coming back to my store," Earl told Justice. "I know I went a little overboard the last time you were in and I've tried to tone things down this time. Wouldn't want you to feel uncomfortable or anything. Hope you don't mind that I called you a Marine hero in front of everyone when you first walked in?"

"I'm no hero," Justice began.

"Sure you are," Earl interrupted him.

Justice felt the familiar sense of guilt creeping up on him, threatening to overwhelm him with darkness, when he heard Kelly's voice in his mind. *You are a hero, but you're also human...the bottom line is that you would have helped that child no matter what because that's the type of man you are. Honor, courage, commitment. They're ingrained in you.*

Yeah, well if that was the case, if Kelly really thought he had so much honor, then she should have known he wouldn't use her as a tool for revenge. The thing was he had let the idea cross his mind a time or two and he'd been too damn stubborn to defend himself against an accusation that was only minimally true. Instead he'd done what he did whenever his emotions were challenged, he'd come up with an immediate diversionary tactic by fighting with Barbie.

He was afraid Kelly had seen his brief flash of guilt and that was what had put the nail in his coffin as far as her belief in him went. He had to get off this island and find her.

"Earl, I have a favor to ask you."

"Sure, just name it."

"I need to get to the mainland."

"The ferry comes tomorrow."

"Yes, I know. I need to leave today."

"There some problem? Some medical emergency?"

Justice sighed. He'd already been down this road with the scrawny ferry guy and the turtle lady. "Look, Earl, can I talk to you man to man?"

Earl propped his thumbs beneath his suspenders and drew back his shoulders proudly. "Absolutely."

"It's Kelly."

"Your wife? Is she sick? Does she have a medical emergency?"

What was it with medical emergencies and this group? They seemed to have a thing about them. "No, she's already left the island."

"Oh. She's already left." Earl nodded with the understanding of a man of the world. "You two newlyweds had a spat, huh?"

Justice wasn't about to deny being married to Kelly. At this point he just wanted to find her ASAP. "Something like that."

"I remember when Tilly and I were first married…" Earl launched into a lengthy story that Justice listened to as long as he could before interrupting him.

"What about a boat, Earl?"

Earl scratched his chin before shaking his head regretfully. "Well, the thing is, we've got this race going on now…"

"I know, but there must be some kind of boat you could use to get me back to the mainland."

"There is one," Earl admitted, "but I don't think it's suitable for a man like yourself."

"Trust me, Earl, I don't care what kind of boat it is."

"Can't you wait until tomorrow to talk to Kelly? Call her or something?"

Justice shook his head. "This is something I have to do face-to-face."

"If you're sure…"

"I'm sure, Earl."

"Then I'll take you myself."

"Thanks, Earl. I owe you one."

"Don't thank me yet. You haven't seen Neptune's Folly yet.

When Justice did see the boat he almost didn't believe his own eyes. He'd undertaken missions from mighty aircraft carriers in the Arabian Sea, from Coast Guard cutters off the coast of Alaska, from Chinese junks in Shanghai. Even so, he'd never seen anything like this.

From starboard to port, the entire aft of the craft was covered in some sort of crepe-paper-adorned arbor, with a giant silver spear sticking out of the top. Perched on the cabin cruiser's prow was a big-breasted wooden figurehead that would have made Blackbeard proud. It looked like something from a floating bordello.

"I've got her dolled up for the Neptune's Folly boat parade tonight," Earl explained. "Got me first place last five years in a row. Step carefully now. Don't want to disturb Big Bertha up there." Earl nodded toward the voluptuous and nearly naked figurehead.

Big Bertha, indeed. Kelly would have found this entire situation very amusing. Too bad she wasn't here to enjoy it with him.

"Welcome to your new home, Chocolate," Kelly said as she opened the front door to her town house.

The place looked different to her. She looked around. Nothing had changed. The plump ivory couch with raspberry chenille throw pillows was still the focal point of the living room off the cathedral ceiling foyer. The pair of hibiscus plants near the sliding door were blooming, the flowers a vivid pink that picked up the colors in the large oil painting over the couch—a beach scene meant to depict the coast of Italy. The painting reminded her of the beach on Pirate's Cove. She could almost hear the hypnotic sound of the surf, feel the warm, soft sand beneath her bare toes.

Looking down she saw ivory carpeting beneath

her feet and Chocolate spread out on that carpeting, his muddy feet testimony to the rain that had fallen shortly before their arrival.

Okay, so she'd have to make a few adjustments. Ivory carpeting might not be the best choice here. She could change that. Dark brown wouldn't show the dirt as much.

She headed for the kitchen, bringing Chocolate with her. The hallway was tiled in eggshell ceramic squares and would be easier to clean than the carpeting. The dog clearly liked the kitchen, heading straight for the shiny white fridge.

"Your food isn't in there, it's in here." Kelly set the bag of groceries on the small pine table that she'd picked up at a local flea market.

Chocolate checked out the equally shiny fronts of the dishwasher and stove before returning to Kelly's side to investigate the bowl of dried dog food she'd set down for him. He ate a few of the nuggets before looking up at her reproachfully as if to say, "These aren't leftovers. Where's my lasagna?"

"This is dog food. It's what you're supposed to be eating. I left the lasagna back on the island, okay? I can make more, but don't think it's going to be your main meal. Those days are over. You're starting a new life now." She reached for the paper towels and dampened one before belatedly wiping the dog's paws. "Maybe I should just put you in the shower," she muttered. The memory of the last time she'd given Chocolate a bath set her back on her heels. Justice chasing her after she aimed the garden hose at him, Justice telling her he had a terrible ache, Justice kissing her as if there was no tomorrow.

But tomorrow had come, and with it had come

the heartbreak of knowing that he'd only been playing a cruel game with her.

The fates were playing a cruel game with him. Justice had decided that much when it had taken him hours to find a car to rent because of some kind of big tourist event in Beaufort. Just his luck that rain had started to fall as soon as he drove north to Nashville and continued all night. Just his luck that a semi had jackknifed, closing one lane of the interstate and backing up traffic at the start of Nashville's early morning rush hour.

His shoulder throbbed painfully by the time he arrived on Kelly's doorstep, a sharp reminder of how he'd come to be here and the journey he'd taken to arrive at this point. He'd had plenty of time to think during the long drive, plenty of time to work on what he was going to say to Kelly when he saw her.

This time he had a plan. As Kelly had said, a Marine usually had a plan. Something else she said once kept coming back to him, as well. When he'd told her she was sexy, she hadn't believed him. She'd told him that she wasn't the kind of girl who gets the guy.

Well, all that was about to change. She was exactly the kind of girl for this guy. And he'd tell her so. He just wasn't sure how. He wasn't at ease with fancy words the way his brothers were. He'd never been a smooth talker. Fact was, he'd never been much of a talker at all. He preferred to have his actions speak for him.

Which meant taking Kelly in his arms and kissing her the moment she opened the door. Only problem was, he had a feeling she'd slug him if he tried it. No, first he had to explain things to her, convince her that while he may have briefly considered using her as a way of getting back at Barbie, it had only been because he'd been suspicious of her motives in helping him, in kissing him.

Okay, so that was his plan. First he'd briefly explain, then he'd take her in his arms. Or at least his good arm. And he'd tell her about his plans for their future. Good. That sounded like a plan.

He looked for the doorbell, finally finding it on the wall at a right angle from the door. Stupid place to put a bell. Maybe he should have combed his hair or shaved or brushed his teeth or something first. Too late now. Where was she? A car he assumed to be hers was in the driveway, which meant she was home. It was still too early for her to be out.

He rang the bell again. He heard the sound of a dog barking on the other side of the door. The aforementioned canine had noticed his arrival. He noticed she didn't have a peephole on her front door. He'd put one in for her.

Finally he heard the sound of the dead bolt being undone.

Sweat pooled above his lip, and his palms were damp. Ridiculous. He'd faced death unafraid and here he was, scared of a little thing called love.

The door opened. Kelly stood there, her hair tousled, her Tennessee Titans sleepshirt sliding off one bare shoulder, her big brown eyes looking at him as if he were the scum of the earth.

"What are you doing here?" she demanded in a frosty voice that was still husky from sleep.

"I came to see you."

"What for?"

"To talk to you." Brilliant, Wilder, he mocked himself. Tell her, tell her why you're here. "I came to tell you…"

"There's nothing you could tell me that I'd want to hear."

She tried to close the door in his face, but he moved quickly to put his foot out, preventing it from slamming. "Kelly, listen to me, this is important. I drove all night to tell you…" The words froze in his throat, not because he didn't love her, but because he did. Not because he didn't mean the words but because the words meant so much. He swallowed and started again. "To tell you that…that…that I…I…I love you."

Chapter Eleven

"Is this your idea of a joke?"

"No," Justice replied, taken aback by her accusation. "It's my idea of a romantic declaration." Clearly he'd done something wrong here. This was not the reaction he'd been hoping for.

During the long drive up he'd envisioned her falling into his arms, and the two of them making love. Apparently that wasn't going to happen this second. Maybe he should have worked more on that speech the way his mother had advised him to.

"Look, I don't know what kind of devious plot you've come up with this time... What are you grinning at?" Kelly demanded.

"*Devious*. It's one of those words you use like *trifled with* and *trouncing*. That's one of the things I love about you. Your prodigious vocabulary."

She eyed him suspiciously. "Have you been drinking?"

"I wish," he muttered, starting to feel like an

idiot. "I don't suppose you have any whisky in the house, do you?"

"No. And even if I did, there's no way I'd invite you in for a drink. Not after what you did to me."

"You're talking about what your sister said." Justice knew he'd have to address that matter sooner or later. He'd just hoped it would be later. "It wasn't true."

"Right," she scoffed. "*Now* you say that. Now when you're trying to reel me in like some fish you've got on a baited hook. Well, I'm not a fish."

Justice blinked at her, baffled by this turn in the conversation. "Right. I know you're not a fish," he said carefully.

"And I'm not taking the bait."

"Look, I'm really not much of a fisherman, so could we cut the fishing references here?" he asked. "I'm trying to tell you that I love you."

"Stop saying that."

"I thought that's what you wanted to hear."

Uh-oh. Big mistake. He could see the fury flaring in her eyes.

"How like a man to say something simply because he thinks it's what a woman wants to hear." Her sharp words dripped ice.

"That's not the only reason I said it."

"I don't believe you."

"Marines don't lie."

"Of course they do," she shot back. "Especially if they're Force Recon Marines and lying will get them their objective."

She watched the light in his blue eyes dim. "I'm no longer a Force Recon Marine."

She found herself almost reaching for him before

remembering where that had landed her last time, in his arms, half-naked. She sighed. "Justice, I don't know how to help you."

He stiffened his shoulders. "I didn't come here looking for help."

"Then why did you come here?"

"I already told you…"

"And I told you that I'm not buying your claim that you love me. So why don't you tell me the real reason?"

"You're impossible, do you know that?" he growled in frustration.

"Thank you so much for sharing," she retorted.

"Do you love me?"

His point-blank demand left her speechless.

"Well, do you?"

"I'm closing the door now," she said.

"Wait. You don't know what I've gone through to get here. I was on a boat with Big Bertha."

"Then maybe you should show up on her doorstep instead of mine."

Slam.

Justice hadn't even gotten to greet the aforementioned canine, who had docilely sat at Kelly's feet and stared at him in commiseration.

A Marine never surrenders. Which meant it was time for plan B—calling reinforcements.

When the phone rang later that morning, Kelly fully expected it to be Justice demanding once again to know if she loved him. Instead it was her father, demanding to know if she'd lost her mind.

"What were you thinking, going off to help your sister's ex-husband that way? After all the things he did to her.'' Roger Hart sounded outraged. ''Instead of thanking his lucky stars that she married him, he took off with the Marines, abandoning her.''

''Justice didn't abandon her, Dad. She grew bored when he didn't make her the center of his universe.'' She heard her father sputter on the other end of the phone.

''I can't believe you're taking his side in this.''

''Dad, their divorce was over ten years ago. It's time to move on.''

''That's what Mrs. Wilder said when I called her, but—''

''Wait a minute,'' Kelly interrupted him. ''You called Mrs. Wilder? When?''

''Yesterday. I remembered hearing something via the grapevine about the Wilders moving to the Phoenix area so I took a shot and called information down there.''

''You had no right to do that.''

''I had every right. I was worried about my daughter.''

''You were worried about Barbie, but you've got two daughters, not just one.''

''I know I've got two daughters.''

''Really? Because you don't often act like it. You always take Barbie's side in any issue, because she's the beautiful one and I'm only the smart one. Talk about playing favorites. I've been quiet about it in the past, but I'm not going to sit here and let you harass Mrs. Wilder because of your mistakenly placed loyalty to Barbie. Mrs. Wilder has been a good friend to me over the years since Mom died, she's been there for me more than you or Barbie have been.''

Her announcement was met with a stunned silence at the other end of the line.

"I'm sorry," she said more quietly. "I didn't mean to get all emotional like that."

"Have you and Barbie been fighting?"

"No, actually we had a wonderful talk yesterday and cleared the air."

"Because I've gotta tell you," her father continued, "I feel like I've stepped into the Twilight Zone. You've always been the dependable one. It's not like you to fly off the handle this way."

Kelly rolled her eyes at Chocolate, who was lying at her feet on the kitchen floor. Oh, yeah, she'd always been the dependable one, and look where that had gotten her. In a mess. The bottom line was that she needed love as much as the next woman. She just wished she'd chosen someone else to love, someone without a track record with her sister.

"So shoot me if I don't want Justice Wilder hurting my youngest daughter the way he did my oldest one." Roger's voice was becoming increasingly agitated. "Shoot me for being a father concerned about *both* his daughters. Yes, I said both and I mean both. Okay, so I may not be the most demonstrative person, but you're both my kids—I care about you, and I worry about you."

"I'm fine, Dad. You don't have to worry."

"Good. That's all I wanted to hear." Kelly had to smile as he quickly went on to change the subject to something less personal, talking about his business trip to California. He'd recently left his middle-management position with a multinational company to become a business consultant. Like Justice, her dad avoided emotions if at all possible.

So why had Justice come to her front door claiming he loved her? A Marine hates to lose. That was another fact. Maybe she'd hurt his pride when she'd walked out on him. That had to be it.

Even if Justice did think he loved her, Kelly didn't think she was ready to open herself up to him hurting her again. She couldn't believe his emotions for her were serious. Not the way they'd been for her sister.

By the time she'd said goodbye to her father, she'd reached the decision that the sign above her kitchen sink referred to her relationship with Justice as well as to her life at the moment: "Nobody said it would be easy, but this is ridiculous."

She'd told Justice she didn't do easy, that she liked a challenge. At the moment, easy looked very appealing for a change.

The phone rang again. This time is was Mrs. Wilder. "I just spoke to my dad," Kelly said. "I'm so sorry if he gave you a hard time."

"He was just concerned about you. I could understand that. I told him that Justice wouldn't hurt you. I'm sorry that wasn't the case." The older woman's voice was filled with regret and sympathy.

Kelly blinked away tears. "How much do you know?"

"Only that you wouldn't have left the island ahead of schedule if something hadn't gone wrong, like Barbie showing up."

"What did Justice tell you?"

"My oldest son barely said two words beyond the fact that he wanted your phone number and address. I gave them to him, but only after making him promise he wouldn't hurt you again. He cares about you, Kelly. He might not be able to say the words…''

''Oh, he said the words all right. Showed up just after dawn this morning on my doorstep announcing he loved me and demanding to know if I loved him.''

Mrs. Wilder sighed. ''When I told him to work on a speech, that wasn't what I had in mind. What did you say?''

''That I didn't believe him.''

''Justice won't have liked that.''

''He said he thought I wanted him to say that he loved me, so that's why he said it.''

Mrs. Wilder groaned. ''I had no idea he was so romantically inept. But, hon, I think he really does love you. He's always been one to believe in actions over words. He doesn't give me flowery cards on Mother's Day, but he always sends me a big bouquet of my favorite red carnations without fail. He did come after you, Kelly.''

''Because a Marine hates to lose.''

''I don't think that's the reason.''

''You're his mom, it's your job to think the best about him.''

''True,'' Mrs. Wilder admitted. ''But you're my friend, and it's my job to tell you the truth.''

''Even so, your first loyalty is going to be to Justice and I can understand that.''

''Give him a chance, Kelly. I know you don't want to get hurt again, but give him a chance to explain why he did whatever it is you think he did.''

''I gave him the chance when we were still on the island and he didn't say a word in his own defense.''

"Was Barbie there?"

"Yes," Kelly admitted.

"Well, that probably affected his common sense."

"Don't you see, I don't want a man who is still so deeply affected by my sister. I want someone who'll love me for myself."

"I understand. And I think Justice is that someone. Give him one more chance, Kelly. Don't close the door on your future happiness without doing that much. I'd hate for you to look back years from now and regret that fear held you back from reaching for your dreams."

"I must be dreaming," Joe Wilder said. "This can't be my oldest brother, Justice, calling me for romantic advice. Being an expectant dad must have affected my hearing."

"Shut up," Justice growled into his cell phone. He was holed up in a discount motel fifteen minutes from Kelly's town house. Maybe after he got some sleep, and some advice from his married brothers, he'd be more successful dealing with Kelly.

Joe hooted with laughter. "No, this is too good to let pass without marking the occasion."

"Forget it. I'll call Mark instead."

"No way." The Wilder brothers were very competitive. "I can give you better advice than Mark can."

"He courted a princess."

"I courted my commanding officer's daughter," Joe reminded him. "Much harder to do. Hey, what are you doing!"

A second later Justice heard his sister-in-law, Prudence's, voice. "Don't ask Joe for any romantic advice," she told Justice. "Your brother doesn't have a clue. You need a woman's perspective. What seems to be the problem?"

"My wife is bossy," Joe called out in the background. "Have you noticed that?"

"I'm also pregnant with your child and dealing with morning sickness so don't mess with me, Wilder."

"Sorry," Joe and Justice both said in unison.

"I meant that comment for my husband," Prudence said. "So talk to me, Justice."

Kelly was bossy, too. Maybe Prudence was right, maybe it would be better to get a woman's perspective on the situation. So he laid out the facts as best and as briefly as he could.

"Barbie walked in on you and Kelly kissing, and when she accused you of using Kelly to get back at her you didn't defend yourself? Why on earth not? Bad move. Very bad move."

"Tell me something I don't know," he growled before remembering she was pregnant and should be spoken to politely. "Look, there's no point in rehashing the past. I need advice on where to go from here."

"I'll say you do. Just showing up on her doorstep and saying you love her...that sounds like something Joe would do. But it's not enough, Justice."

"So you're saying...what? That I should have brought flowers and candy as well?"

"That's not going to do it. You have to explain your actions to her."

"She slammed the door in my face."

"When I wouldn't listen to Joe, he kidnapped me

from the school where I teach. Swept me right off my feet.''

Justice frowned. "You liked that?"

"I hated it. The only good thing about his idea was that he made me listen to him. Good luck, Justice, I need to go eat more saltines now. Morning sickness. Talk to you later." She handed the phone back to Joe who closed with, "One more thing, big bro. Never give up. Fight for the woman you love, it's worth it in the end."

Justice called Mark next, who was much more sympathetic to his quandary. "Hey, I'll be the first to admit that I don't understand the female mind," Mark said. "And I never thought love would get me. I told myself I didn't do love."

"Me, too."

"I mean, we're guys, we don't talk about that stuff. About touchy-feely stuff like emotions."

"Yeah, I know." Justice had always kept his innermost thoughts and emotions tightly locked up, believing they shouldn't be tampered with. And now look at him. Calling his brothers and talking about personal stuff instead of sports.

"But then you meet *the* woman and she opens up the whole can of worms."

Mark's reference to worms reminded Justice of Kelly freeing the worm she'd named Fred along with his crawly cohorts. He remembered the light in her eyes as she smiled at him that day. He'd probably fallen for her right there and then, only he'd been too stubborn to admit it.

"So how did you convince your wife that you loved her?" Justice asked.

"For one thing, I asked her to marry me," Mark replied.

Marriage. For once the concept didn't make Justice's stomach plummet. When he'd talked to Kelly about most women not understanding the demands of being married to a Marine, she'd told him to wait for a woman independent and strong enough that she wouldn't have to depend on him being with her every second of the day. And when he'd asked her if she was a woman strong enough to be married to a Marine she'd said, "Absolutely."

She was such a jumble of contradictions, sure of herself in some ways and uncertain of herself in others—most notably in her ability to be seductive. Justice wanted to change that. He wanted to woo her, to make her feel special. And he wanted to win her, to bed her, and yes…to marry her.

"How did you propose?" he asked Mark.

"I got down on one knee in the garden behind her father's palace and asked her. I was wearing my dress blues uniform at the time. I started out with a dorky Prince Charming costume earlier that night, which should have convinced her without my saying a word that I loved her. But women seem to want to hear the words, so I would go with that and forget the costumes. I dumped the costume ASAP. The dress blues uniform added a nice touch, though. But, hey, like I said, I'm no expert. Maybe a grand romantic gesture would be better."

"Or maybe I should cover my bases by doing both—go with the romantic-gesture thing and the spilling-my-guts-talking-to-her thing."

"Sounds like a plan to me," Mark said. "Good luck and let me know how it goes."

Justice had a plan, all right. A few more phone calls should put it into action....

Justice arrived at Kelly's house the next afternoon. Today he took the time to notice his surroundings. The neighborhood was quiet and well maintained. Unlike many developments, this one had a number of mature trees in the area, including one in her compact front yard. A kid's bike lay on the driveway next door and the smell of newly mowed grass was in the air. And there, tied to the tree in her front yard, was the aforementioned canine, who looked up and greeted Justice with what he could have sworn was a doggie grin.

"At least *you're* glad to see me," Justice told the dog, rubbing one of the animal's floppy ears. "I still say Chocolate is a silly name for a dog. Devil dog would be good. That's a nickname for a Marine, you know. Not that you have what it takes to be a devil dog. No, maybe you're better as A.C." He used the abbreviation for aforementioned canine. "So fill me in here, A.C. Do you think Kelly will be more receptive today? Do you think she'll listen to me this time? I spent half the night trying to come up with a fancy speech and all I ended up doing was sounding like an idiot. So I'm just going with the truth. And the truth is that I love her."

Woof.

Justice rubbed the dog's other ear. "Yeah, I know it sounds pretty lame, especially after I talked to my brothers and asked for their advice. I'm sure they'll hold that over my head for the rest of my days. Me, the oldest one, making a fool of myself over a woman. But she's not just any woman, as you know, A.C. She's pretty damn special.''

Woof.

"I know, I know. Swearing shows a lack of discipline. Don't tell her about my momentary lapse. It'll be our secret. I couldn't believe she took you with her when she left. I should have known she would, though. She'd already told me that she would never abandon someone she loved. She left me pretty darn fast, though, which made me wonder if maybe she didn't love me after all.

"But then, well, let's just say we shared some stuff before her sister walked in on us...Kelly isn't the kind of woman who'd do that if she wasn't serious about a guy. Can you believe she doesn't think she's sexy? How idiotic is that? I mean just looking at her makes me hot. Her smile burns me up. Remember how lean and hungry you were when you first came to the beach house? Well, that's how she makes me feel. Being with her makes me feel...complete, I guess. Sounds sappy, I know.''

Justice paused to glance over his shoulder at her front door before turning his back once more and continuing. "She'll probably laugh at me when I try in my stumbling way to tell her all this, to tell her again that I love her. And then she'll probably kick me out, but I'm not giving up. If any woman is worth fighting for, Kelly is. Because she's special, and she's definitely worth waiting for. You know when I knew it was serious? I knew she was trouble from the moment she showed up on my doorstep in that storm.

"And, okay, so I admit that for a brief moment I did consider the fact that she might be using me as a way of getting back at me for the divorce with her sister. And because of that, I thought about the possibility of using her before she used me. But that went out the window the first time we kissed. I should have told her that when Barbie walked in on us and started hurling accusations around like hand grenades. But I panicked.

"Dumb I know, but there you have it. I'm not trained in handling situations like that. Going behind enemy lines, that I can manage. But this emotional stuff, well, I'm doing the best I can here because I do love Kelly and she means more to me than…" His throat tightened and he couldn't get the words out. It took him a moment before he could gruffly continue. "Well, let me put it this way A.C., I realized that Force Recon is no longer the most important thing in my life. Kelly is. And that pretty much says it all."

"Yes, it does," Kelly said.

Justice whirled around to find her standing a few feet behind him. He noticed that her formerly closed front door was now open.

"How much of that did you hear?" His voice was rusty and his stomach felt greener than when he'd been stuck in a force-nine gale off the North Sea in a small fishing boat.

"All of it. I was upstairs. My bedroom window faces the front of the house and I had the window open. I heard you drive up, I heard you talking to A.C., and I heard you say that you loved me."

"I told you that yesterday."

"Not the way you told A.C. today."

Nothing he could have done would have convinced her that he loved her or made her feel more seductive than overhearing his rough confessions to her dog, an animal Justice had tried to keep his distance from. The walls she'd built since leaving the island had come tumbling down around her, leaving her with two unalterable facts—that she loved Justice and that he loved her. Everything else could be worked out if those two facts were true.

And she was willing to believe he did love her. It had been there in his voice, even if he had been talking to Chocolate instead of to her. And it was there now, in his eyes. Had it been there yesterday, and her anger and pain had blocked her from seeing it? She wasn't sure. She only knew that no one had ever looked at her this way, as if she were the center of their universe, as if she were more important than air, as if she were a precious resource to be protected and cherished.

Justice was also staring at her as if unable to grasp that she wasn't ordering him off her property or threatening to call the cops on him. "You don't think I planned it this way, hoping you'd overhear me?"

"Did you know I was upstairs?" she asked.

"Hell, no. If I had, then I wouldn't have made such a big fool of myself by talking to a dog like I did."

"Which is what I figured."

"Yeah, but I'm Force Recon. We're used to being devious."

"Which is why I know you'd have come up with a better plan than talking to Chocolate."

He nodded. "Good point. As for Force Recon, you made me realize that I needed to concentrate on what I have, not on what I've lost. So I talked to my C.O. this morning about instructor duty to prepare other Marines for Force Recon. He thought the idea had a great deal of merit.''

''I'm glad.'' She knew how important the Marine Corps was to Justice, it was as much a part of him as his blue eyes or his rare smiles.

''I meant to court you, to woo you. I considered sweeping you off your feet like my brother Joe did with the woman he loves, but that's not going to happen with my bad shoulder. So then I considered making some sort of grand romantic gesture like getting some buddies who were former members of the Marine Corps Band to serenade you with your favorite song. Nashville is Music City and these guys work here because they're musicians. Then I realized I didn't even know your favorite song.''

''It's a tie between Faith Hill's *This Kiss* and *Breathe*,'' she said with a smile that made him believe this might work out okay.

''And then I thought how pitiful is that, not even knowing Kelly's favorite song? But I know so much more about you. Like the fact that you know stuff about Spanish moss and Blackbeard, that you're always learning, that you prefer the red M&M candies over the green ones, that you like comforting others but somehow don't think you're worth being comforted yourself. You are, you know. I love you for who you are, for all your strengths and stubbornness. I love you because you make me a better man. So then I thought maybe the situation wasn't so pitiful after all.''

Blinking away tears of happiness, she moved closer and put her hands on his chest. He was wearing another one of Striker's Hawaiian shirts. The cotton was soft, wrinkled and warmed by his body. "You know what I think?"

"No, what?"

"That it's about time you kissed me."

His mouth found hers in a kiss that was a merging of souls as well as lips. She'd once told him she wasn't the kind of girl that got the guy, but he was clearly set on convincing her otherwise. He told her without words that she was the most seductive woman he'd ever met, that touching her was a slice of heaven, that she possessed a feminine power that matched his masculine need.

It didn't matter that she was wearing her oldest pair of running shorts, or that her T-shirt was thin from so many washes in the machine. It didn't matter that she wasn't wearing makeup. Every electrifying stroke of his tongue against hers, every erotic thrust of his hips was a physical expression of his love for her.

Exhilaration raced through her veins as she responded. Fluid and feverish, she melted against him, her heart beating like a huge drum. Vaguely she realized that wasn't her heart, someone was playing a huge drum. In fact, there were a number of someones, enough to make up an abbreviated version of a marching band heading up the street and directly into her driveway. She broke away from Justice in astonishment.

"Uh, I guess in all the excitement I forgot to cancel the grand-romantic-gesture band thing."

She had to laugh at his sheepish expression. "Is this what life will be like, married to a Marine like you? Filled with unpredictability?"

"Affirmative," Justice replied, cupping her cheek

with his good hand. "But the one thing you can always count on is my love for you."

Once again tears welled in her eyes. "Oh, Justice…"

"I was going to wait until later tonight, after taking you out to some romantic place for dinner, and I was going to be wearing my dress blues uniform…oh, what the heck. I can't wait any longer." Taking her hand in his, he dropped to one knee, there beneath her maple tree, there beside her dog. "Kelly, will you marry me? I won't lie to you, we both have strong wills, and being married to a Marine isn't the easiest thing on the planet."

She placed a trembling finger on his sexy lips. "I already told you, I don't do easy. I know it won't always be smooth sailing between us. But I also know now that what we have is worth fighting for, despite the complications. So, yes, I will marry you, Justice Wilder. Not because you serenaded me with a marching band, but because you've entrusted me with the most precious thing of all—your love and your heart."

Epilogue

One Year Later

"**I** can't believe this day has finally arrived," Kelly said.

"Your wedding day." Mrs. Wilder smiled at her in the mirror.

"And everything is coming together just as planned. The weather is perfect...all our friends are here. Justice and I have come full circle. We're back where it all started. At Striker's beach house on Pirate's Cove, about to get married on the beach. With Chocolate acting as our flower dog."

"I don't know how you trained him to carry that basket of flowers so well."

"He's an exceptionally smart dog."

"The dress rehearsal yesterday went quite well."

"Aside from Chocolate bumping into Big Bertha."

"An unusual wedding decoration, I must say," Mrs. Wilder confessed with a laugh.

"That half-naked figurehead helped bring Justice to me."

"So you both have said."

"When he first told me he was on a boat with Big Bertha I thought the worst. I told him he should show up on her doorstep instead of mine."

"I'm so glad you and Justice worked things out."

Kelly turned to hug the older woman. "Have I told you how much I appreciate all you've done for me over the years? Not the least of which was sending me out here to look after Justice."

"And you've been looking after him ever since."

"We've been looking after each other. Justice has done as much for me as I have for him. He's made me a believer in myself in ways I never thought possible."

"I'm so glad." Mrs. Wilder blinked away tears.

"Don't you start," Kelly warned her, wiping at her own eyes. "We've already redone my mascara once."

"That was because you and your bridesmaids had a laughing fit reading those medical jokes."

"A gift from my co-workers at the hospital who couldn't be here today."

"I'm so glad you settled in so well in Norfolk."

"So am I." Kelly had continued working in Nashville until Justice had been deployed to the Little Creek Naval Amphibious Base in Norfolk, Virginia, after his medical leave. She'd taken a job eight months ago at a Norfolk hospital, where she fit in as if she'd been there for years. Julie Mc-Murphy and Cleo Penn were her bridesmaids, co-workers and friends. Both were in the other room, waiting for Kelly. "The thing I miss the most is my town house in Nashville, which is why I've rented it instead of selling for now. Justice proposed to me beneath the maple tree out front."

"Moving frequently is one of the downsides of marrying a Marine," Mrs. Wilder said. "I've lost count of how many times we've moved over the years."

"I've learned to deal with the unpredictable. Like my sister getting pregnant with twins. They're due any minute now, which is why she couldn't attend the wedding. Actually she confessed that she was worried Justice and I would get married before she did and steal her thunder, so to speak, and was so relieved when we didn't do that."

"Has she accepted your relationship with Justice?"

"I think she has. I know my father has, although it has taken time."

"Where is he? Shouldn't he be here with you since it's almost time to start?"

"He said he wanted to talk to Justice for a minute."

"So we're understood?" Roger Hart stared Justice right in the eye as the two men stood on the beach house deck. "You hurt my little girl's heart and I'll break both your legs, Force Recon Marine or not."

"Understood, sir," Justice said with a smile.

"You're not supposed to smile when you say that, Justice."

"I'm sorry, it's just that every single time I see you, you feed me the break-your-legs line."

"I mean it each time."

Justice nodded solemnly. "I know you do."

Mr. Hart slapped him on the back in an awkward sort of hug that guys did. Quickly moving away, he added, "Did I tell you I appreciate not having to dress up in a tuxedo for this wedding?" Roger was wearing a summer-weight suit.

"I believe you did, yes."

"Whose idea was this beach wedding thing?" Roger asked.

"Kelly and I both agreed on the idea."

"Good answer." Roger nodded approvingly. "I do believe you two are going to be okay."

"You can count on it, sir." Justice's voice was confident.

"You look mighty calm for a man about to tie the knot," Justice's buddy Striker noted as he joined them. All three of Justice's brothers were close behind, all but Mark were in dress blues uniforms, as was Justice.

"Maybe he's sleeping standing up," Mark said.

"His eyes are open," Joe pointed out.

"Force Recon Marines know how to sleep with their eyes open," Striker retorted.

"You boys about ready to get this show on the road?" The booming question came from Justice's dad, Bill Wilder. He had a drill instructor's voice and a warrior's demeanor. His graying hair was cut short in a high and tight Marine cut even though he'd retired from the Corps several years ago.

"Affirmative, sir," Justice said with a grin.

"I'll go tell your mother, then. She's pulling double duty today, mother of the groom and matron of honor.''

"I'm sure she's up to the job," Justice said as his dad and Roger headed inside.

"Don't forget proud grandmother," Joe added, as his wife, Prudence, joined them with their five-month-old baby boy, Matt.

"Whenever I see so many Marines huddled together, I know they're plotting something," Mark's wife, Vanessa, declared as she joined them. Justice had missed both Mark's wedding and Joe's, because he was on missions. He was glad his entire family was able to join him, although it had taken some maneuvering to find a date when everyone was available. The wait was worthwhile.

"We're plotting a wedding," Mark said, after kissing his wife.

"I love the idea of a beach wedding," Vanessa said. A former European princess who had renounced her claim to the throne in order to follow her dream of working with orphaned children around the world, she still possessed that regal authority that was as much a part of her as her blond hair.

"Hey, I never thought of that, but a beach wedding is a perfect place for a Force Recon Marine to get hitched," Striker noted. "After all, we've been trained in beach reconnaissance and surveillance tactics, as well as clandestine entry and extraction."

"Big Bertha's presence on the beach kills any chance of us being clandestine," Justice noted wryly.

"Not many people can pull off having a seminude figurehead at their wedding, but I think you and

Kelly can make it work," Vanessa said with a grin. "Who knows, if I'd seen Big Bertha sooner, I might have had her at our wedding."

"Right." Mark laughed. "She'd fit right in at the Volzemburg Royal Chapel."

"She could keep all those gilded angels company," Vanessa replied.

"Speaking of company, I think we should go join the minister, because it looks like it's time to start," Sam noted.

"In a few minutes you'll be the only remaining single Wilder brother," Justice noted.

"And I plan on making the most of that, believe me," Sam said with a grin.

Justice had asked Striker to be his best man, not wanting to choose one brother over another for that job. Besides, Striker knew him better than anyone else. Mark and Sam were standing up with him, partnering Kelly's two bridesmaids. His buddies from Nashville who'd done the marching-band thing in Kelly's driveway were performing in a more traditional way here, having left the marching bass drum behind this time.

White chairs had been set out for the guests, which included Earl and his wife as well as Marge, aka turtle lady, and her husband. Many of the guys from Justice's Force Recon squadron were present as well. He'd expected to be more nervous about today, but all he felt was an overwhelming sense of this being right.

There were peach-colored roses all over, hanging from the arbor where they would exchange vows as well as decorating the chairs along the aisle…and, of course, surrounding Big Bertha.

Chocolate performed his duties with gleeful precision before sitting beside Justice to wait for Kelly.

When the wedding procession music started, Justice thought he was ready. He wasn't. Kelly simply took his breath away. She'd kept her wedding dress top secret. He could see why. She looked unbelievably beautiful in a simple ivory satin strapless gown. The pearls he'd given her were around her neck and her caramel wavy hair was left loose around her shoulders as he'd requested. He grinned as he caught sight of the question mark dangling earrings she'd worn when she'd first come here last year.

Her father accompanied her to Justice's side before kissing her cheek and sitting down. Justice took Kelly's hand in his, unable to believe his luck. She'd threatened to make him write their vows, but had only been teasing. In the end they'd gone with a short ceremony, with each one contributing one line of their own.

"You are my anchor," Justice said simply. "My reason for being."

"And you're my hero, not because of your uniform but because of what's in your heart."

When he slid the simple gold band on her hand, Kelly knew she truly had come full circle.

"You may now kiss the bride," the minister said.

The band played, the Marines shouted "Ooh-rah" in their traditional motivational cry, Chocolate barked with excitement, the guests all applauded—but the only thing Kelly focused on was the feel of Justice's lips on hers. Some things were worth waiting for, worth fighting for, worth working for. A love like theirs was one of those things, something special, something magical.

Oh, yes, she was definitely going to enjoy being married to this tough Marine of hers, the man who'd always held the key to her heart.

* * * * *

Look for

SLEEPING BEAUTY & THE MARINE

*in January 2003,
only from Cathie Linz
and Silhouette Romance.*

SILHOUETTE *Romance*®

Prince Henry's heirs are about to discover the perils of love!

THE CARRAMER LEGACY

Carramer glories continue!
Valerie Parv, official historian to the Carramer crown,
tells the tales of a new batch of cousins
who discover the legacy of love!

**October 2002 (SR #1621)
CROWNS AND A CRADLE**

**November 2002 (SR #1627)
THE BARON &
THE BODYGUARD**

**December 2002 (SR #1633)
THE MARQUIS AND
THE MOTHER-TO-BE**

*Look for these titles wherever
Silhouette books are sold!*

Where love comes alive™

Be sure to visit Silhouette at www.eHarlequin.com   SRCL

SILHOUETTE *Romance*®

presents rising star

MYRNA MACKENZIE's

romantic miniseries

Where the highest bidder wins...love!

Ethan Bennington begins the bidding
in **August 2002** with
BOUGHT BY THE BILLIONAIRE (SR#1610)

Join Dylan Valentine in **October 2002**
when he discovers
THE BILLIONAIRE'S BARGAIN (SR#1622)

And watch for the conclusion to this trilogy
in **December 2002** with Spencer Fairfield, as
THE BILLIONAIRE BORROWS A BRIDE (SR#1634)

Available at your favorite retail outlet

Where love comes alive™

Visit Silhouette at www.eHarlequin.com   SRWA

magazine

♥——————————————————————— **quizzes**

Is he the one? What kind of lover are you? Visit the **Quizzes** area to find out!

♥——————————————— **recipes for romance**

Get scrumptious meal ideas with our **Recipes for Romance.**

♥——————————————————— **romantic movies**

Peek at the **Romantic Movies** area to find Top 10 Flicks about First Love, ten Supersexy Movies, and more.

♥——————————————————————— **royal romance**

Get the latest scoop on your favorite royals in **Royal Romance.**

♥——————————————————————————————— **games**

Check out the **Games** pages to find a ton of interactive romantic fun!

♥——————————————————— **romantic travel**

In need of a romantic rendezvous? Visit the **Romantic Travel** section for articles and guides.

♥——————————————————————————— **lovescopes**

Are you two compatible? Click your way to the **Lovescopes** area to find out now!

Silhouette® —

where love comes alive—online...

Visit us online at
www.eHarlequin.com

SINTMAG

**Where royalty and romance
go hand in hand...**

The series finishes in

with these unforgettable love stories:

THE ROYAL TREATMENT
by Maureen Child
October 2002 (SD #1468)

TAMING THE PRINCE
by Elizabeth Bevarly
November 2002 (SD #1474)

ROYALLY PREGNANT
by Barbara McCauley
December 2002 (SD #1480)

Available at your favorite retail outlet.

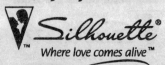

Where love comes alive™

Visit Silhouette at www.eHarlequin.com   SDCAG

SILHOUETTE *Romance*™

**Lost siblings, secret worlds,
tender seduction—live the fantasy in...**

A TALE OF THE SEA

**Separated and hidden since childhood,
Phoebe, Kai, Saegar and Thalassa
must reunite in order to safeguard
their underwater kingdom.
But who will protect *them*...?**

July 2002
MORE THAN MEETS THE EYE
by Carla Cassidy (SR #1602)

August 2002
IN DEEP WATERS
by Melissa McClone (SR #1608)

September 2002
CAUGHT BY SURPRISE
by Sandra Paul (SR #1614)

October 2002
FOR THE TAKING
by Lilian Darcy (SR #1620)

*Look for these titles wherever
Silhouette books are sold!*

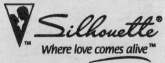

Silhouette®

Where love comes alive™

Visit Silhouette at www.eHarlequin.com   SRTOS

A powerful earthquake ravages Southern California...

Thousands are trapped beneath the rubble...

The men and women of Morgan Trayhern's team face their most heroic mission yet...

A brand-new series from *USA TODAY* bestselling author

LINDSAY McKENNA

Don't miss these breathtaking stories of the triumph of love!

Look for one title per month from each Silhouette series:

August: THE HEART BENEATH
(Silhouette Special Edition #1486)

September: RIDE THE THUNDER
(Silhouette Desire #1459)

October: THE WILL TO LOVE
(Silhouette Romance #1618)

November: PROTECTING HIS OWN
(Silhouette Intimate Moments #1185)

Available at your favorite retail outlet

Where love comes alive™

Visit Silhouette at www.eHarlequin.com   SXSMMUR

SILHOUETTE *Romance*

COMING NEXT MONTH

#1618 THE WILL TO LOVE—Lindsay McKenna
Morgan's Mercenaries: Ultimate Rescue
With her community destroyed by an earthquake, Deputy Sheriff Kerry Chelton turned to Sergeant Quinn Grayson to help establish order and rebuild. But when Kerry was injured, Quinn began to realize that no devastation compared to losing Kerry....

#1619 THE RANCHER'S PROMISE—Jodi O'Donnell
Bridgewater Bachelors
Lara Dearborn's new boss was none other than Connor Brody—the son of her sworn enemy! Connor had worked his entire life to escape Mick Brody's legacy. But could he have a future with Lara when the truth about their fathers came out?

#1620 FOR THE TAKING—Lilian Darcy
A Tale of the Sea
Thalassa Morgan wanted to put the past behind her, something that Loucan—claimant of the Pacifica throne—wouldn't allow. Reluctantly she returned to Pacifica as his wife to restore order to their kingdom. But her sexy, uncompromising husband proved to be far more dangerous than the nightmares haunting her....

#1621 CROWNS AND A CRADLE—Valerie Parv
The Carramer Legacy
She thought she'd won a vacation to Carramer—but discovered her true identity! Sarah McInnes's grandfather was Prince Henry Valmont—and her one-year-old son the royal heir! Now, handsome, intense Prince Josquin had to persuade her to stay—but were his motives political or personal?

#1622 THE BILLIONAIRE'S BARGAIN—Myrna Mackenzie
The Wedding Auction
What does a confirmed bachelor stuck caring for his eighteen-month-old twin brothers do? Buy help from a woman auctioning her services for charity! But beautiful April Pruitt was no ordinary nanny, and Dylan Valentine wondered if his bachelorhood was the next item on the block!

#1623 THE SHERIFF'S 6-YEAR-OLD SECRET—Donna Clayton
The Thunder Clan
Nathan Thunder avoided intimate relationships—and discovering he had an independent six-year-old daughter wasn't going to change that! Gwen Fleming wanted to help her teenage brother. Could two mismatched families find true love?

Visit Silhouette at www.eHarlequin.com   SRCNM0902